"The story Ruth Billings tells in this book is fiction, but what she says about the Philippines, its people, and their culture is factual and telling. She lived and worked in the Philippines for thirty-eight years so has an in-depth understanding of Filipinos and their culture. You will learn much about the country and its people, and how God works in people's lives, as you read this book."

Leonard Tuggy
Former Asia Ministries Director and Philippines Field
Conference Chairman, CBI/World Venture

"Walk with Sue as Ruth unveils rural Philippine life, language, and culture in a riveting read. She has been framing faith-building stories for years, and as her mission colleague I saw them change her audiences as she directed them as stage plays decades ago. The Billings's cultural coaching launched me into a fascinating career serving the adopted people they loved."

Cheryl Forster
Christian Education trainer, Missionary
with CBI/World Venture

"*Abandoned?* is an adventurous tale that is taken from true events. This must read will challenge, encourage, and reassure your life's journey."

Dr. Dax Garlinghouse
Lead Pastor, Baker Creek Community Church

ABANDONED?

A Novel

By
Ruth Billings

Deep River
B O O K S

Table of Contents

Prologue

The Philippines, October 1944

Only once before in his life had Joseph de Cou felt so trapped. That time some kid had pushed him back into the middle of a thick blackberry patch they were picking. It hurt to move. Something crawled along his arms and face. The more he struggled, the more encased he became.

"Oh God, help me!" he croaked out. Nobody else heard him. This time he was alone.

He'd been dumped into what seemed to be a cavern of forest greenery. Vines grabbed at him, branches cut off his view, huge trees with leaves so dense blocked the light that barely crept through. He must be alive. He felt the heat. His clothes stuck to his flesh. He was so thirsty. He moved a hand, searching for his canteen. It took effort to remove the lid, but then he guzzled the water eagerly.

He lay still. He had to think like an adult. Back then he was just a ten-year-old kid picking blackberries to earn money to buy a bike. This was now, life or death, a grim reality.

What had happened? He tried to think. *Oh yes, my plane was shot down.* Jumping out, he'd felt the dizzying spin downward, pulled the ripcord, then nothingness.

He tried wiggling his arms and legs. They seemed to be okay. But why did his head ache? Hunger? He reached into his pocket and pulled out a chocolate bar, now soft and mushy and covered with ants, but delicious. He was still so thirsty. He needed to find water. This place seemed damp enough. But where was he?

He tried to remember the attack. The fighter had unexpectedly appeared on their flank. They had been over the dense forests of the Sierra Madre. The route had been . . . Where was it? Southeast of the Balete Pass.

His mind wandered. What were the steps to survival in the jungle? First, find water. He'd concentrate on that; he was so weak he could only crawl. So thirsty. So exhausted by the intense, humid heat. It was easier to lie down and die. Then he knew nothing more.

﷽   ﷽   ﷽

A week later, once his body had recovered from the crash, but still waiting to be found by the Army's Search and Rescue, Joe cut back some vines with his many-bladed Army knife. He then wove the vines into a circular frame, inserting the edges of his handkerchief to make a coffee-filter-like contraption. Then when the afternoon rains came, he positioned his canteen to catch the rain. Now, he had clean, filtered drinking water. Step One of survival when stranded.

﷽   ﷽   ﷽

The subconscious expectation of cooler weather to indicate that it was now fall never came. Instead, the tropical summer moved into slightly drier days and nights temperatures in the seventies. The summer lingered. He struggled to stay alive in these conditions. The biting bugs and leeches were detestable; the resulting open sores itched and festered. Hungry, he hunted for edible roots. He dug for sweet potatoes and taro. Sweet potato leaves tasted good. Praise God for the bananas so abundant and tasty.

Were there no people in this jungle? There must have been at one time. He eventually found a simply constructed hut, abandoned for sure. Just an enclosure, but it offered protection from the drenching rains and itchy ants. The stench of diarrhea, which so sapped his strength, was always prevalent. He could barely crawl down to the stream nearby to relieve himself or bathe.

At times he didn't feel it was worth the struggle to stay alive. Then he thought of Lois, his loving wife, who made his insistence on survival so necessary. How was she? Their baby girl Sue must now be walking, or even talking. Oh, how he missed them. Then he again mustered his waning strength to drag his weakened body out to find sustenance.

He'd been fortunate that day to find a huge cluster of bananas ripe and low enough to the ground on their broken stalk for him to hack them off fairly easily. The banana diet seemed to help the spasms in his stomach.

His only luxury was being able to use his mind. He was constantly thinking. Didn't the men in his unit try to locate him? Had he been abandoned? How long ago was that? It may have been months, even a year ago. Time had passed in the blur of the struggle to just survive.

He thought of the war—those vicious attacks on the fleeing Japanese up the valley toward the pass, the numerous enemy tanks he saw out of commission on the road north to San Jose. He'd smelled the smoke rising from the burning town of Muñoz. War really was ugly, causing humans to hate their fellow men, and then kill them. He shuddered at the remembrance.

His weakened body and mind wandered back to former times, to a few weeks before the crash. They'd ducked into the bamboo clumps as the Japanese patrol came into view up the road.

"Run," his buddy yelled. "We've been spotted!"

So Joe put on his best fifty-yard sprint in a westerly direction into the denser vegetation. His friends rapidly veered off on another path. Twenty-five minutes later, his side aching, he entered a small clearing. He could hear his pursuers still crashing through the jungle toward him.

Then he spotted the hut. Two old folks and two teenage girls were cooking and tending the water buffalo.

Staggering into their secluded clearing, he gasped out, "I'm an American. Can you hide me?"

"*Dali* [quick], get in here. We'll hide you."

He was pushed roughly under a pile of clothing, pillows, and mats piled in the corner. Even though they were in danger themselves, they quickly concealed him.

The two girls confided in him as they rearranged the stuff. "Grandma warned us that whenever soldiers showed up, we were to hide because they would hurt us. But you are not Japanese. We want to help you."

Then they left the hut to stir the pot where they cooked on an open fire.

Looking through the cracks between the bamboo slats, he saw the two Japanese soldiers who had been pursuing him emerge from the thick vegetation with drawn guns. They were looking for him—their enemy. His blood seemed to freeze in his veins. He didn't want to put this family in danger. They'd been so helpful to him.

Now as the two men approached, the two young daughters of the family huddled together, giggling nervously, but terror was evident in their faces. The girls, frozen in place, kept stirring the pot over the open fire.

The men yelled loudly in unintelligible Japanese. The girls stood trembling. Then the aroma coming from the cook pot attracted the young men. They took off the lid and inspected the thin soup. That day, the last remaining chicken had been caught and killed for this soup. Only a pullet, but that was all the family had. There were few vegetables growing in the dry season. This was the normal diet for these harassed country people in hiding from the occupation army.

With elaborate gestures, the men made it clear they wanted to be fed. They looked into the steaming pot, but it seemed to be nothing but broth. "*di puwede, di puwede!*" they exclaimed in broken Tagalog ["This won't do!"]. Again, by gestures they demanded that those vegetables growing in rows nearby be added to the stew.

The girls shook their heads vehemently, "No!" This denial of their demands made the men become more threatening. Pushing the girls aside, one grabbed up a leafy plant, rung off a few leaves, and threw them in the pot, as a way of demonstrating what he desired. The girls looked horrified. The men interpreted their response as reluctance to comply.

One soldier kicked the nearest girl sharply in the buttocks until she complied and added more of the pungent, inedible leaves. The ravenous young men swallowed voraciously for only a few minutes. They left hurriedly, gagging and retching, from the now bitter soup.

Luckily for Joe, they had forgotten their enemy. Joe's life had been miraculously saved by what he recognized as "tobacco stew."

"Thank you, God, for sparing my life!" he whispered.

Now his mind returned to his unpalatable present. He was alone and seemingly abandoned. But he knew God had spared his life for some reason. As the months passed, his total focus was on the endless effort to remain alive. He thought of Lois. He prayed for baby Sue. He sought God's help for sustenance, water, even the faith to keep going. There was no mental or physical energy left to look for a way out of this impenetrable jungle. This was the northern mountain slopes of the Philippines.

ONE

Searching for Answers

Powell, Wyoming, June 1949

"**M**ommy, what happened to my daddy?" I asked one Father's Day when I was in second grade. "Everyone else but Judy had their dads there today for our program." I had always wondered about the person my dad must have been.

"Sue, honey," Mom answered, "he was in the army fighting the Japanese in the Philippines when he . . ." My mom gulped, hesitated, and then when I looked at her, tears dripped down her cheeks. After that, I didn't ask any more questions about my daddy.

I'd never known my dad, Joe de Cou, because he had been declared missing in action just after I was born. But subsequent odd events seemed to prove he might not have died. I was determined to find out . . . to go on a quest for my peace of mind. I wanted to know for sure what had happened to him.

I planned my research trip to clear up the three-decades-old mystery. I wanted to know where Dad had been all this time. Was he dead, or could he still be alive? Why was there information about him years after his supposed death? And I had to find out who Estelle de Cou was. She'd written about her love for Dad. My mother had never shown me that letter.

My dearest Lois, and little Sue, too   8-31-45

Things seem very tense on the perimeter. I had an interesting incident last night. At the end of my KP duty I was taking out the two huge buckets of table scraps and peelings. A young farmer comes to the gate each night to get these for his pigs. Native pigs are getting fat on U.S. Army leftovers. This night Manuel was acting furtive. We talked a while. "You have wife, ba?" he asked. I nodded yes. "She like pretty . . .?" Lost for the right word in English, he loosely circled his neck with his finger and made a circle around his ring finger. I understood him to mean jewelry. I again nodded yes. I knew you liked pretty things, Lois. I was wondering where this conversation was going. "You buy pretty hikaw?" He pinched both his earlobes. I understood him to mean earrings. I again nodded. He glanced nervously around. "Here, you buy for her. Very special." Watching intently, I saw him unwrap a piece of newspaper. In spite of the dirtiness, I could see they were intricately made. These are unusually lovely pieces. Yes, you would like them. I paid him 100 pesos, and we were both pleased. "Don't talk," he whispered, with a finger to his lips, and then he left with his pig food. This seemed a bargain to me.

When I returned to the barracks, I polished up those earrings with my toothbrush and toothpaste. They shone like real gold. You'll love them, Lois. I wonder if they are antiques. I put them in my wallet to bring to you.

Later that night there was a fracas outside the gate, and we heard that Manuel had been attacked and killed. All the slops were strewn around, to the delight of many dogs and children, I'm sure. I was sorry to hear that. I'd enjoyed my few times with that young man. I have a busy flight tomorrow, and I'm exhausted from this job.

All my love,   Joe

In fact, she had never shown me any of my dad's letters. I only found them after she died. I sadly looked at Dad's last letter to mom.

I wanted to know what actually happened during those dreary war months of fighting in Nueva Ecija Province and my dad's apparent missing-in-action status.

Then that strange phone call. I wondered about my mother's unexplainable silence about it. Now that my mother was no longer alive, I decided to look for my own answers. So here I was in the Philippines in the country where my dad, Joe de Cou, had disappeared.

This was my first trip abroad. I'd been born in Wyoming and lived there my whole life, except for my college years. After my husband passed away, my friends advised me to get away from Powell and the constant reminders of my mother and Bob.

"Take a trip. Go somewhere," they all said.

My mom had been my strength after Bob died. Now even she was gone. This mystery of not knowing what had actually happened to my dad plagued me. So I decided to plan a trip to Asia. I'd always wanted to know the truth about my parents' marriage. Now was the time to take positive action.

§   §   §

That's how I found myself sitting in a luxurious hotel room in Manila, Philippines, the furthest I'd ever been from Powell, Wyoming. The air conditioner hummed and blew welcome cool relief to chase away the soggy heat outside. My total disorientation and confusion bewildered me. My fuzzy thinking resulted from twenty-two hours of sitting on the plane, but only catching a few moments of sleep. My weariness magnified my attention on the cool sheets that awaited me in that nicely made bed. Soon my plans to take immediate action on my quest blended into restful sleep. Forgotten was the exhaustion. Forgotten was the lost feeling at the airport. Forgotten were the strange languages, the enveloping heat, and my delayed baggage.

I woke to the phone ringing, and ringing, and ringing. *No one knows I'm here! Go away!* I decided to just let it ring and put a pillow over my head. But finally, the persistent ringing and my normal curiosity won out. I picked up the receiver.

"Hello." My voice sounded hoarse with sleep. Squinting at the number on my room key, I added, "Room 311."

A strident voice demanded, "Jan, where's that information we wanted! Did you bring it?"

"You must have the wrong room. There's no Jan here." I dropped the phone into its cradle in disgust. Who, pray tell, was Jan?

This trip was the culmination of so many small incidents: my natural curiosity about my dad and the thick bundle of letters from him that mom had kept, but never shown me. These old letters had been hidden in a large brownish envelope in the back of my mother's file cabinet. I wondered why she had never shared them with me all my growing-up years. She had really not talked much about her husband, the man who was my dad, and this fact puzzled me.

I cried for the first time the day I read those letters They were tears for a dad I could only know through his letters: his war friendship with those he met during his stint in the US Army in this country; and his description of the frustrating heat and the defiant and determined enemy—men who never were willing to give up until they were dead. Fighting, evading, hiding. As I read those thirty-year-old letters, I wished I could have known him. I wished I could have known what really happened to him.

I wasn't able to get the strange phone call out of my mind either. Mom had taken scratchy notes on a piece of paper and then taken care to circle the charge on that "collect call" from a place called Cabanatuan, Nueva Ecija in the Philippines dated May 24, 1951. A call cut off at only one minute.

"Joe *deetoe*," Mom had scribbled. ". . . very seek . . . she die . . . no walk." Then Mom had added, "Didn't get the name of the caller, a man, who seemed to speak very little English."

Didn't make any sense to me at all. But the fact that this note was carefully placed with letters from Dad must have meant that Mom was puzzled and wanted to keep the evidence.

I had delayed going through my mom's stuff after her death. Just going into her room made me depressed. I wasn't surprised to find that my mom had kept Dad's letters, but it was many months after her death that I found them. I opened the first letter in the bundle and read:

My dearest Lois,

I didn't feel I could sleep without you next to me. I was so lonely those three weeks on board ship. The others, also lonely men around me, made it seem less severe. Then landing here ashore. I saw women, pregnant women, reminding me of you. I long to hold your bulging figure. I want to feel our baby kicking inside this bulge. Oh, Lois, I miss you so much. I must mail this immediately. The pouch is closing now. XXXXX OOOOO

All my love,   Joe

My dear wife, Lois,

I still have to get used to the different weather patterns here. Not realizing how virulent and sudden tropical storms could be, we ducked under the awning of a little store. With us were several other young men, also seeking shelter from the downpour. I heard, "Hey, Joe" right behind me, my head swiveled like that of a horned owl. "Do you know me?" I asked. This seemed be a joke as the fellas laughed. I was confused. Later I found out most Americans are called "Joe" here. A really friendly place, if your name is "Joe." Truly, I have found Filipinos to be so approachable, easy to talk with, in spite of the pressures and fears of the war going on around us. It's been an adjustment trying to understand the heavily accented English. Lois, you should come back out here with me, after this awful war is over. You would also enjoy these lovely people.

All my love, Joe

As I wiped a tear running down my right cheek, I could only imagine the love my mom and dad had for each other. My own widow's heart spoke.

Oh, Bob, I'm lonely for you too! We enjoyed ten years of our great meeting of minds, emotions, and pleasure together.

I continued opening a few more letters from my dad and my lonely pain increased. Reading these old letters brought out longings I thought I'd carefully buried and forgotten.

I wondered if pondering these love letters should best be forgotten. But I was also motivated by a need to know. Each letter brought more tears as I opened yet more and wept more. I was moved by his descriptions of the rigors of tropical living, the heat, and incessant mosquitoes. I was attracted to the people he described. Each letter talked of mom's pregnancy with me. I turned the air forms over to see what the dates were. Mom had kept them in order.

The first one was September 1942. I ruffled it open to see the date—September 15. Mom must have been only four months pregnant with me when Dad left. I suppose during those years when she had wondered what had happened to him, she'd read them over and over. I'm sure they were a means of comfort during the uncertainty, and yet she had never shared these with me. Why?

Then the letter dated March 15, when he knew he had become a father. He drew little bows up the side of his writing to say hi to his new little girl, me. He talked of longing for a son next time. That would never be. He was declared missing in action just two years later.

At that point when I read his letters, the first seed of a plan began to form in my mind. I wanted to go and see the places Dad mentioned. He related visits to the famous Catholic cathedrals that must be centuries old. His descriptions of brief friendships with the delightful and welcoming Filipino people inspired me to get to know them too.

With this curiosity as stimulus, the perusal of the mail seemed less traumatic. I looked to see where Dad had gone. I didn't find many towns mentioned; maybe he could not mention place names when fighting a war. Apparently, he went north from Manila. We always used "up" to mean "north." Dad had written, "I went up to the place we were to be billeted, almost a swamp. The rain fell every day, heavily."

Actual descriptions of war skirmishes were noticeably absent, I suppose due to censorship, or maybe not to worry my mother. But the everyday coping with the heat, and the uncertainty, and longing came through clearly as he wrote almost every week.

Occasionally a clipping from the newspaper, or *Time* magazine, was enclosed with the letter. My mother must have done this. These US articles stated places, battles, and casualties in vivid detail. I picked up the last of Dad's letters.

TWO

The Heat

Manila, July 1980

As I strode through the lobby, I heard a greeting I didn't understand. I paused and glanced back and saw who I thought must be a hotel employee. He looked like a young boy dressed up for a part in the school play. His uniform was bright blue and orange and a size too small. I acknowledged his greeting and smiled. *Possibly the bellhop?*

Determined to discover this new world, I walked eagerly out of the hotel into the brilliant tropical sun. *Feels like a sauna!* Perspiration beaded on my arms and forehead, and I felt something crawling down my spine. Couldn't dislodge that critter, and then I discovered it was sweat running down my spine. In a matter of minutes my blouse stuck to my skin. The sun seemed unbearably strong, and now I knew why I had seen so few people walking about. Those who did carried open umbrellas as protection against the sun's intense rays.

Is this what Dad felt like here in the Philippines? Was he wet with sweat constantly? I was sure there were no air-conditioned quarters in wartime, like the cool air in the hotel I'd just left. I dug into my shoulder bag for a hanky but mopping my forehead didn't help much. I knew I wouldn't find out much if I stayed in the coolness of the hotel, but this humidity and heat felt unbearable.

I hadn't envisioned I would be hindered by such unrelenting heat. The fishy smells wafting down little alleys bothered me as well. Curious little boy vendors followed me down the block, trying to sell me one stick of gum, one or two cigarettes, or maybe a menthol candy. They seemed determined that I buy something from them. I was horrified to see a man, his back toward me, urinating against a wall. I was embarrassed, but he didn't seem to be. Maybe it wasn't such a good idea to take a walk after all. Having only gone a block, I turned around and returned to my hotel.

In Powell, Wyoming, walking a few blocks would be a pleasant stroll. Wyoming was so different from Manila, its dry and cold weather a stark contrast to this rainy and steamy heat.

My hometown in Wyoming was set out neatly, streets evenly spaced apart, with orderly traffic. Manila seemed like bedlam in comparison. I hadn't thought I'd survive the taxi ride from the airport with hundreds of vehicles all vying for position in laneless traffic. Pure havoc!

Shaking myself, I muttered, "But at least I'm actually here."

Visiting the tropics was like stepping onto a different planet. How did others get around without cars? I would have to ask at the hotel.

I'd been overfed on the plane from San Francisco, but now I felt really hungry again. My mind wandered. *So this was the life of a tourist.* I strolled into the coolness of the hotel lobby, breathing a sigh of relief as the cool air washed over me again. However, I wasn't accustomed to affluence. The home I'd lived in with Bob was like most of the other homes in Powell, not pretentious, but it was all Bob and I had wanted during our years of marriage. This hotel embodied luxury itself—employees everywhere, soft carpets under foot, soothing music coming from some lounge around the corner.

I recalled the loneliness after Bob's death when I had made the decision to move into Mom's house. Afterall, she needed someone with her, and her presence kept my loneliness somewhat at bay. We amicably settled into double widowhood in her large home. I had my own apartment, but we ate meals together. I remember one conversation we had.

"Mom, why don't you ever talk about my dad?" She hadn't been expecting this question, so it took her a few moments to answer.

"Honey, it was hard to face when I was young. Then as you grew up, I pushed the pain away. I just couldn't face the fact that your dad wasn't coming home. It was just easier not to bring up that subject."

I wondered why it was so painful for her. When I asked questions, though, she would evade them, or clam up.

But now, in a foreign country surrounded by all these people, I hoped I might get some answers. I had no doubts about the wisdom of embarking on this crazy quest. I needed a plan, though. My main aim for being here was to find out what happened to my dad. My search resulted from the many mysterious, unexplained events. Why the strange phone call? Dad had been declared missing in action in 1945, but someone phoned Mom many years later. She never mentioned the phone call to me, probably because it didn't make sense.

Among the pitiful few pieces of evidence that puzzled me was the other letter mailed six years after his supposed death. It was written on notebook paper and said, "I love Joe. He means everything to me. He is too sick and weak to walk. I'm so sad. I want to go to college at CLSU–Estelle de Cou."

The letter had been sent in an envelope made of cheap, brownish paper, now old and faded. I could hardly make out a postmark. A 'C' then 'tuan' plus 'N' & 'E,' I thought.

My mother had written on the outside. "Got this letter six years too late! Who could this woman be?!"

In my hotel room, I laid the letter on the bed but then changed my mind and put it back in the folder. I again looked at my dad's picture—a good-looking young man. Only twenty years old, he sent it to Mom before being shipped overseas. Included with his letters were his service number, company, and division. That was the paltry bit of information I had to follow a thirty-year-cold trail to find my dad.

My growling stomach reminded me again that I was hungry. I took a shower, and it felt so refreshing. My feet were puffy and swollen and barely fit into the only pair of sandals I'd brought with me. Putting on my coolest blouse and cotton skirt, I prepared to leave my room. Placing my purse straps over my shoulder, I paused and remembered the intense lecture I received when I picked up my passport at the US Embassy in San Francisco:

"A US passport is a very valuable commodity overseas. When stolen this document can be sold on the black market for thousands of dollars. Carry it on your person at all times. Preferably use an inside pocket. Do not put it in a desk drawer, a hotel bedside table, or in a purse left on a table. If you are a tourist, keep your passport with you at all times, Never, never leave it in your hotel room, apartment, or home unless you've placed it in a secure place like a safe or locked file cabinet."

I was tempted to leave my large purse in my room, but remembering that warning, I removed my reading book and the large envelope with dad's letters. Then I placed them in the bed-side drawer, shouldered my purse, and descended by elevator to the lobby. Enquiring about some place to eat, I was directed to the restaurant called El Niño, which was a tastefully decorated room with lush tropical palms and potted philodendrons that provided privacy between tables.

Looking at the menu, I didn't know whether to be adven-turesome or not. I pointed to *pancit* on the menu, and then hesitantly, I asked my attentive waiter what was in this dish.

"Bits of fried pork, noodles, sliced Baguio beans, *cahhrots*, and cabbage," he said. Then he added, "You like it. Americans like it." The *pancit* was truly delectable. It was a unique way to combine pasta, meat, and vegetables, and the added juice of one little lemon-lime added a nice tartness to cut the pork fatti-ness. My waiter said the little green lemon-lime-type fruits were called *calamansi. Cah-la-MAN-see* was the way he pronounced it. I was having fun!

The person at the next table had a bright orange-yellow fruit for dessert. I asked what it was. "Mango," he said, so I ordered one for myself. Even the way it had been sliced was unique. Split open on each side of the flat seed, the outer "cheeks" were crosshatched and then splayed open, skin side down, over the seed section. It tasted refreshingly tart, but with a sweetness like a peach. I decided I would enjoy mangoes often here.

Glancing around, I had the feeling I had drawn a lot of attention. Obviously, I was a neophyte in the experimental stage of discovering new foods. It couldn't be because I was beautiful. I'd never considered myself overly attractive. Bob's compliments on my "glistening brown hair and clear skin" I had attributed to husbandly bias. True, I did appear to be rather pale in contrast to the natural tans of the many Filipinos eating there. Was white skin an attracting factor? I was to find out this assumption was true in this country.

Filipino men and women deserved my admiration. Dressed impeccably, their clothes were tailored to fit them perfectly. I felt they had just the right amount of tan. Their dark, almost black hair was combed to stylish perfection. I was sure the average US hotel would not have this many good-looking, well-dressed people on an average evening. My impression was that Filipinos cared how they looked. There were very few overweight customers. Since they were dining in this luxurious restaurant in The Manila Hotel, I didn't suppose that could be contributed to poverty.

As I stood to leave, I felt tall at five feet six, and I was inches taller than the waiter. I'd never felt this tall in my life. My optimism rose, probably due to my now full stomach, the friendly atmosphere, and the fact that I'd finally arrived at my destination. My dream that had taken ten months of planning and saving had been fulfilled.

I took the elevator back to my room, determined to make specific plans for action tomorrow. However, the fact that I was a single American woman traveling alone was a huge drawback. All my plans made in Wyoming seemed to melt into the exhaustion of jet lag. With only enough energy to pull off my clothing, I dropped gratefully into bed—again. But I was glad I had arrived.

THREE

Treasure Hunters

Manila, 1980

A lthough the tensions of war were over, intrigue and dark schemes surrounding it still lingered. The whole country lived in a fever pitch of treasure hunting. The retreating Japanese had been chased by the Philippine-American Army, but the enemy had managed to hide all their stolen loot before escaping north through Aparri.

Millions of pesos in jewelry, gold bars, antiques, artifacts, and gold-plated idols had been pillaged from wealthy residents and even the churches and cathedrals. Often rich landowners would buy their freedom to continue rice farming by giving up their Spanish antiques, knowing that even the Japanese needed rice to eat.

Now, two men—Sonny, who was about thirty-two, and one older man, Cesar—were intent in their pursuit of this treasure. In fact, that was why they hung around in the hotel lobby the day Sue arrived.

Sonny spoke just above a whisper. "What can we do now? I didn't expect Jonathon to give up so easily. He was our last chance to find out where Yamashita hid his treasure. Jonathon

27

Henry was right there, he admitted that, but escaped unnoticed under cover of darkness. I couldn't get him to divulge any more information."

"There's not much we can do about that. Where was Jonathon's little girl that night?" Cesar asked. "I don't really know, but I do know Jonathon told me, 'My daughter knows the facts!'"

Both men were silent for a minute, looking around to see if there was any eavesdropper close by.

"Jonathon's daughter, Jan, is due to arrive this week to claim her dad's body," Cesar said. "I think we should leave a note at the hotel desk, saying we want to meet with her. Do you think that will work?"

Sonny shrugged. "Maybe. We can try." He grabbed some hotel stationery from the desk nearby and wrote, "*Jan Henry, we are sorry to hear of the loss of your father. May we meet with you upon your arrival about a matter of vital importance? Just leave a note for me at the hotel desk. Sincerely S. Agraviador.*" He showed the note to his companion, who nodded. Sonny placed the note in an envelope and left it at the hotel desk.

The next morning, Sonny read the answer she had left at the desk. "*I will only meet with you if you have fifty-thousand pesos in your hands for me. We both know what this is about. J.H.*"

Amazed, Sonny turned to the desk clerk and blurted out, "When did this note come to you?"

The desk clerk looked at the other hotel employee behind the counter for confirmation. "I believe it was passed to us about midnight last night."

Sonny frowned. *We've missed her! Now what?* Discouraged, he slumped into a rattan chair and scanned the room.

A casual observer would not have noticed the brown-haired woman enter the lobby. She was pretty, but not outstanding.

Her white skin was very attractive, though. The diffident way she moved seemed appealing. Sonny watched her.

She must be unsure of herself. Jan had driven such a hard bargain and asked such a phenomenal price for her information, Sonny presumed she'd be more businesslike—more hardboiled. He thought she'd have a firmer set to her mouth and would wear more makeup.

This woman looked like the girl next door, as Americans said. Oh, but she wasn't! She wanted fifty-thousand pesos for her information. *We knew she was the only surviving relative of Jonathon Henry, and now here she was.* Sonny didn't necessarily expect a beauty contestant. But this woman exuded innocence. She must be a fantastic actress. Sonny followed her with his eyes and noticed a well-formed figure, healthy-looking but not overweight. She must be thirty years old or so. She should be older than that to be Jon's daughter.

"We were dumb not to get a physical description of Jan," he muttered to himself.

Sonny felt an angry flush creeping over his face. This female walked through without even looking for him, not making eye contact with anyone. He couldn't believe it!

Taking a chance, Sonny strolled over to catch her name as she registered at the desk. Maybe he could make contact with her in a less crowded place. The clerk handed her the key.

"Your room, Mrs. Gibson, is number 311. Enjoy your stay with us. The bellhop will take your bag up for you."

Our valuable contact entered and ascended in the elevator without a single glance at him or showing any vestige of curiosity. She was traveling under an alias too. This Jan was one smart cookie. He decided to call her later. He took out an old sales receipt and scribbled her room number on the back, then inserted the bit of paper back into his pocket.

Sonny casually strolled outside to meet again with Cesar, the man who knew how to deal with crooks like Jan. He arrived at Cesar's hovel, out of breath and sweating profusely, but making a victory sign with his fingers.

"Is she the only American woman to check in alone at that hotel this week?" Cesar inquired.

"I just can't believe she is our contact," Sonny said. "She didn't seem at all curious about her surroundings. She didn't look for me. If she *is* the one, she's a clever actress—slippery as a snail."

"We can't lose this evidence to someone else," Cesar growled. "Once we know the correct location, we'll be rich men for life!"

"We'd do well to search her room," Sonny said in his quieter, more educated voice. "We'd recognize the information from Nueva Ecija. Besides, it wouldn't cost us fifty-thousand pesos to get this information." He chuckled.

"Okay, Sonny, go over and watch for her to leave her room," Cesar said. "You got her room number, I hope. Report back here at noon tomorrow."

Sonny left to catch the common means of transportation, a renovated army jeep elongated to seat twenty people and decorated lavishly to express personality. This was the only means of transportation for an overcrowded and poor populous. For Sonny, a jeepney ride to The Manila Hotel was a regular occurrence.

Early the next day, Sonny saw his chance. He noticed a woman, who was rather overweight, struggling with many filled shopping bags, getting out of a taxi. He presumed she was the kind of woman who came to Manila to spend money lavishly, then dress extravagantly to impress the other women *sa provincia*. Sonny gallantly offered his help in the absence of the bellhops. They mounted the steps, and Sonny helped her with her bags and rode the elevator up to her third-floor room. The fifty-peso tip was an unexpected bonus since he felt he'd been done the favor. He had gained access and only needed to find the correct room—Jan's room—which he had been told to search.

As Sue ate a leisurely breakfast in the hotel's coffee shop that morning, Sonny methodically searched her room. When he saw the brown envelope addressed from Nueva Ecija, he knew he had struck gold. So he slipped the envelope holding all the old letters under his shirt and left the hotel by the back stairs.

FOUR

Temporary Luxury

Manila, July 1980

Twelve hours later, no longer feeling the confusion of jet lag, I awoke refreshed, ready to face my day. The coffee shop seemed the best place for breakfast. Enticed by the French sidewalk cafe decor, attractive pastel color scheme, inviting arrangement, and large floor to ceiling windows that looked out into the garden, I sat down at a small wrought-iron table. I admired the brilliant orchids and ornamental plantings right outside.

After ordering coffee, I contemplated the various options available for breakfast. This was definitely not the standard American bacon and eggs breakfast I wanted. Instead, the menu offered spaghetti or fried rice, as well as *dinuguan* and *puto*, whatever that was. Breakfast wasn't a time to experiment with new and different foods. I wanted two fried eggs, wheat toast, and sausage.

I looked around at the few people eating there that morning. There was an older Caucasian couple at another small table—definitely tourists. They had even brought their cameras to the breakfast table.

Then I noticed a good-looking young man, who smiled at me as I entered. He seemed to have just finished his coffee and stood to leave shortly after I arrived.

Despite few diners, plenty of waiters stood around talking to each other and combing their hair. Apparently, there wasn't a labor shortage in this country. But in spite of numerous waiters, the service was slow.

After a five-minute wait, I bought a newspaper from a young boy who came in with an armful of English newspapers. Strange. No international news was featured on the front page. President Marcos and his wife dominated every article. There were two pictures also. One was a construction project belonging to the First Lady, and then one was President Marcos admonishing the people against conspicuous consumption.

Finally, on an inside page, I found the US news I sought. Most of the comics were in English too. I laughed at *Nancy and Sluggo, Dennis the Menace,* and *The Flintstones.* I'd already read them before in the States, but they were still amusing.

Thinking about the things I had to do today, I scribbled in the margin of the paper—American Embassy, Avis Rent a Car, cheaper hotel rental, look up the name de Cou in the phone book, form a plan of action.

Finally, a waiter delivered my breakfast to the table. I was disappointed. The eggs weren't hot. The toast was limp, cold, and tasteless in contrast with the sausage that was spicy hot and definitely delicious, oozing with grease, but too much so for breakfast. Well, so much for my familiar American breakfast. Denny's this was not!

"Do you have mangoes this morning?" I asked. That would be delicious again. That hour passed leisurely as I ate another juicy mango and drank more coffee. In the newspaper, I read about the continuing hunt for Yamashita's treasure. Apparently, the Japanese had hurriedly hidden their loot when escaping the country before the American victory. Now the exact location of this treasure was the dream of every treasure seeker in the country. Just like me, the intrigue of the unknown was a lure to many adventurers.

I must have chuckled out loud. Heads turned. It was hard to get used to being stared at. *Was I that foreign looking?* I wondered if my dad felt this way too. He had been only a little taller than I at five foot, six inches. In the few grainy pictures I had of him, he seemed to have a darker complexion. Maybe he had blended in better than I seemed to be. But, of course, during wartime there wasn't much blending, communing, or befriending.

I especially remembered one letter Mom got from Dad shortly after he arrived in the Philippines. He'd written:

My dear wife, Lois,

I still have to get used to the different weather patterns here. Not realizing how virulent and sudden tropical storms could be, we ducked under the awning of a little store. With us were several other young men, also seeking shelter from the downpour. I heard, "Hey, Joe" right behind me. My head swiveled like that of a horned owl. "Do you know me?" I asked. This seemed to be a joke as the fellas laughed. I was confused. Later I found out most Americans are called "Joe" here. A really friendly place if your name is "Joe." Truly, I have found Filipinos to be so approachable and easy to talk with, in spite of the pressures and fears of the war going on around us. It's been an adjustment trying to understand the heavily accented English. Lois, you should come back out here with me after this awful war is over. You would also enjoy these lovely people.

All my love,   Joe

My eyes puddled a little as I thought of the person my dad must have been. Coming out of my reverie, I paid the bill and hurried upstairs to my room. Fumbling with my large hotel key holder, I walked noisily down the carpeted hall. What luxury to have someone else make my bed and put clean towels in the bathroom. But as much as I enjoyed this luxury, I wanted to find a cheaper place to stay.

Sitting down on the bed, I pulled the phone book toward me to call other hotels. I wondered if there could be some sort of guesthouse that would be cheaper than this five-star hotel. The US Embassy seemed a logical place to ask. After looking up their number, I dialed. No one answered after six rings. Glancing at my watch, which was still on US time, I wasn't sure if it was office hours here or not.

I opened the Bible next to the lamp, and my eye was caught by something someone else had underlined in red. *"Do not be anxious about anything, but in everything, by prayer and petition, with thanksgiving, present your requests to God. And the peace of God, which transcends all understanding, will guard your hearts and your minds in Christ Jesus."*

Normally, I wasn't a worrier. My faith in a God of peace had enabled me to stay calm in all events. I'm sure someone else had also received comfort from that verse at some time in this lonely hotel room.

I again dialed the embassy number. Again, no answer. I opened the bedside drawer for my envelope and dad's papers. Something was wrong! I was sure I'd left dad's letters in the drawer.

But they were gone!

FIVE

The Jungle

The Philippines, 1944–1949

Kenneth MacLeish described the Philippine virgin rain forest in an August 1971 *National Geographic* magazine article titled "Help for Philippine Tribes in Trouble":

People have lived in Mindanao's forests since the first Malay migrants reached the Philippines . . . they are hunters and gatherers. They spear and trap wild pigs and deer and monkeys, and collect roots and honey and edible leaves and insects. To grow their domestic crops—corn, upland rice, sweet potatoes, taro—they slash and burn small clearings, farm them until the rains have leached away the good of the soil (usually in three or four years) and then move on.

"We waded in silence up the lovely water course where cool clear water swirled over smooth stones. Butterflies glittered over the tumbling ripples. Dark tree trunks rose naked and unbranching to a hundred feet or more and vines hung from the lofty canopy. The filtered light that reached us was an emerald radiance. This is the most perfect forest I've ever seen.

*   *   *

In a similar locale, hundreds of miles north of Mindanao and decades earlier, Sue's father found himself in an immensely difficult predicament.

*   *   *

The rain forests were home to half of all the living animal and plant species on the earth. Very lush, but luckily for Joe, almost inaccessible for typical human use. Two thirds of all flowering plants and herbs could be found there, and Joe sought to eat the ones he recognized. At times he discovered hives of wild honey, which kept him alive a little longer.

Eventually, Joe became almost feral—bearded, hairy, fiercely defensive, wily, and agile. In his stronger moments, he was able to stalk unwary birds or lizards. He became adept in using mud to stave off insect bites. Even as his appearance and demeanor deteriorated, his soul more often sought his Maker, who even then was looking down upon this hapless example of His creation. Joe conversed with his God all through the misery, loneliness, and passage of time.

"God, this seems to be the end. I can no longer keep going." Joe sank down on his coconut-leaf sleeping mat, ready to give up. The pockets on his military uniform had become so tattered, he had tied his wallet to his dog tags.

Who needs a wallet here anyway? He was about to toss the soggy mess but stopped when a morbid thought came to mind. *It would identify my corpse.*

He tied his dog tags and wallet together, then as a final gesture, placed them between two bamboo slats overhead—his tombstone.

Even as Joe sank to a new low, lying in a stupor in his little borrowed hut, the owner of that temporary dwelling wended his way through the dense forest, becoming more puzzled. The root crops he expected to harvest seemed less abundant than usual. Who had been poaching on his territory? Maybe a Japanese holdout. The war had ended years earlier. But there were still soldiers hiding in the dense forest, unaware there was now no more reason for hiding. This forest-wise man knew someone had been here since his visit several dry seasons previously. He sensed he'd come upon the encroacher, as his nostrils reacted to the stench of death.

The human he came upon was just a skeleton and hardly breathing. He didn't look Japanese. The shriveled look and satin-tight features were more Caucasian than Oriental. The tattered clothing seemed to be tan. Whoever he was, this inert being still lived.

Several days later, the strong young farmer staggered into his isolated clearing, carrying the man he'd rescued, the warmth of his body sustaining the ebbing life of the other.

"Lucia, hurry and cook up some ginger and sweet-potato soup!" he called. "I have a man here who is barely alive!"

Using the age-old wisdom of natural herbs, leaves, and fruits, this small family hand-fed Joe back to health. Then they shared their few pieces of clothing.

As his health returned, so did Joe's desire to contact his wife, his little girl, his unit, even civilization. But this bare-subsistence family didn't even own a pen or pencil. The love and acceptance by this simple family amazed Joe. Dorong and Lucia, who possessed little, still gave willingly.

Joe came to love their little three-year-old girl. He poured out his love on her in the absence of his own child. Teaching her how to speak English and how to write gave him a creative outlet. They had to use the dry-packed earth as their blackboard, but it sufficed. She learned to count and to recognize colors. It was by this simple means that Joe could benefit his adoptive family. The little girl otherwise would have little chance of any formal education at all. He, in turn, learned their Ilocano language. He and this family spent their spare hours conversing. At first, hesitantly, in the darkness without electricity, they talked about life, homes, and experiences. They talked of a God who is in charge of every life.

"I know God had you find me for some special purpose," he said once.

The one thing Joe yearned for most during that time, those months of physical convalescence, was some paper to write to his wife. His wish came true when Dorong returned from his annual two-week trip down to Gabaldon. He'd sold his most recent gleanings of sweet potatoes, bananas, peanuts, and bamboo. And he had purchased one small notebook and two pencils for his daughter's new school and teacher.

SIX

Panic

Manila, July 1980

My eyes opened wide in panic. *My dad's letters are gone! I can't believe it.* In utter desperation, I searched all the drawers. Maybe I'd placed them elsewhere. The letters, the folder—all my information was gone! But where? I asked the front desk to send up the maid who had cleaned my room.

"I not touch it, Mum. I honest. I not get money."

I assured the terrified young girl I wasn't accusing her.

"But there was a folder in this drawer when I went down to breakfast, now it isn't here," I explained. "The folder is very important to me. Did you see it?" My request came across as blame. The girl was speechless, shaking, and so scared she'd lose her job. I placed a reassuring hand on her shoulder. "Thank you for coming. Did you see anyone else come into my room?" She shook her head in helplessness. I let her go.

I felt as helpless as that maid. I put my head down on my hands as tears oozed through my fingers. How could I continue now?

Discouraged and searching for some solution, I thumbed through the initial pages of my Bible still on the table. My eye caught the words, "Search for a wife." Reading on down the twenty-fourth chapter of Genesis, I realized the story nearly paralleled my situation.

This man had to go to a far country to search for a wife for Abraham's son Isaac—a girl he didn't know. I received strength from Abraham's predeparture advice to his servant: "God will send his angel on ahead of you, and He will see to it that you find a girl from there to be my son's wife."

This was the same God I knew. He could also go before me to find Estelle. He could help me find out what had happened to my dad thirty years previously. I cried again. I prayed for God's direct guidance.

Now that all my records were gone, there was only one place where I could replace the information I needed about Dad's service time here. I determined to visit the US Embassy. Remembering how hot it was on that first day I arrived, I took a taxi waiting in front of the hotel. Soon I arrived at the embassy, a mile or two down the waterfront from my hotel.

I wondered what I would find in the records at the embassy. But for sure, I wasn't expecting the crowds in front of the gate. *Is this a demonstration I should avoid?* No, apparently just quiet lines. No anger. Just people, waiting. I passed easily into the cool interior where I stated my intent to the guard. Walking down the clean, cool corridors settled my mind.

"What can I help you with?" the receptionist asked.

"My father was . . ." What was he? He was just the daddy I never knew, the man far away at war that mom never talked about when I was little. I was having a hard time expressing myself. *I better get realistic and get out his service information.* Wait! That was missing too! My mental block was relieved by an understanding question?

"Was your father in the US Army?" she inquired.

"Y-Y-Yes," I stammered. "He fought here in the Philippines."

"Do you know his company? Why don't you give me his name for a starter, then we can see how I can help you?" I felt more encouraged already.

"His name was Joseph Armstrong de Cou—that's D-E, space, C-O-U. He was stationed here from September 1942 to 1945. It was sometime in October when he was reported missing in action.

I was unable to think—shaken. My most important papers were gone. The hands of a thief had effectively erased my chance of success. A quick heaven-sent prayer, "Lord, help me!" calmed me some. I breathed deeply.

She asked sympathetically, "What do you want to know about your father Joseph de Cou?"

"Would you have some file on him? I need information as to his company, where he fought, where he was declared missing." I swallowed the lump welling up in my throat. I didn't want to tell her about Estelle. "You see, we received . . . I mean, my mom received a letter from him several years after his . . . after she thought he was dead."

Tears were close to the surface. She said, "Wait here a moment. I'll look up that name in the files. I may have to go down into the archives. Do you have fifteen minutes or half an hour?"

"Yes." I had all day; I even had all week if necessary.

I sat down. Only twenty minutes later, she returned with a thick file and handed it to me across the counter.

"You can photocopy any pages you desire from that file, but please return it to me."

Opening the cover, I again saw the picture of my dad—the duplicate of the one that had been stolen. Our features were

quite similar. I glanced through the pages of technical information: date of enlistment, vital statistics, and resume. I hadn't
known my dad had a degree in agronomy. He had been with the
37th Infantry Division, stationed at Gapan, Nueva Ecija. Then
I found the paragraph which most interested me:

> *"When declared Missing in Action, their plane, which
> left Kiangin, was making an inspection sortie looking
> for a company of Japanese holdouts, thought to be in
> the dense forest area east of Cabanatuan City. A faint
> S.O.S. was heard about that time; no fix could be made
> on the radio signal. Then no further signals. No crash
> had been reported. After a week of searching for the miss-
> ing plane, it was presumed the plane had crashed in the
> dense jungle between the Central Luzon plain and the
> Pacific Ocean. No further information was ever received
> on the missing plane, its pilot, engineer, and gunner."*

I sat there stunned. *What a way to go! My dad! Was this the
end?* Then I recalled there had been a letter written after this
missing-in-action information.

Having selected the pages concerning his stint on Luzon, I
asked for copies to be duplicated. Handing back the file, I was
optimistic. Again I had some places and facts to follow. The
phone call to my mother from that man had probably come
from Cabanatuan. I remembered the postmark on the letter had
a "C," and then a blur followed by "tuan." I would have to find
out the location of Gapan, Nueva Ecija. If it was close to Cabanatuan, I could probably hire some kind of vehicle and go there.

I decided to walk leisurely back to the hotel so I could
think and decide on a plan of action. I opened the umbrella

I'd brought to shade me. On the way, I wandered down to the breakwater at a lovely park, enjoying the breeze off Manila Bay. Seeing a little stand with Coca-Cola signs, I stopped to purchase a cold bottle plucked from an ice chest. I glanced at the T-shirt clad man as I purchased the Coke.

"Are you an American?" he asked.

"Yes," I replied.

"Are you here just for a visit?"

"I . . . I . . ." I didn't know if I wanted to say why I was here. "I just came a couple of days ago. I may be here a month or so, touring around."

"Where are you planning to go? What would you like to see?"

I shrugged, noncommittally. "What sites would you recommend?" I asked.

"Most Americans like to go to Baguio. It's cool up there." That sounded very appealing. "Up north the Banaue rice terraces are a world-famous attraction. You can take a bus right up there, stay overnight, and come back the next day."

"How long would that take."

"Five or eight hours up, depending on the road conditions and the weather. The road up the mountain slides out when there is a heavy rain."

"You seem to know a lot about it."

"I'm Sonny, a tourist guide at The Manila Hotel, just up the street."

"Oh, that's where I'm staying for a day or two."

"If you'd like to tell me your room number, I'll bring you some tourist brochures later today."

"I'd really appreciate that. My room is . . ." She thought rationally for a minute. "Leave them at the front desk for me.

I'll be there . . . let me see . . . after two o'clock." What a pleasant surprise! I'd have to buy a map to see where I wanted to go. If this man could show me where to get a bus, that would be really helpful.

It was noon by the time I got back to the hotel. Stopping at the bookstore/novelty shop, I asked about a Philippine map. Then the salesgirl showed me where Nueva Ecija Province was. Cabanatuan City was right in the middle of that province.

Later, sitting down to lunch, I looked through my Xeroxes again. Opening the map, I inspected the little names of towns. I was pleasantly surprised to find that Gapan was just south of Cabanatuan. My panic subsided, and I realized God had truly sent an angel to help me get answers.

SEVEN

The Search Starts

Manila, July 1980

Looking dapper in his ironed jeans and collared shirt, Sonny sat with me in the lobby, looking through the ten or more pamphlets that he'd brought. I hadn't realized how many lovely tourist places there were to visit.

"I'd like to go north someplace," I said cautiously.

Sonny quickly got out the multi-colored brochure about the cool scenery of the summer capital in Baguio. He said everyone wanted to go there. He handed me the pamphlet with the pretty Filipino girl on the cover.

"Here's the information about Baguio. You'd like it up there, Jan."

I did a double take. "How did you know about Janet? She and I planned this trip for months, but she backed out at the last minute. How did you know about her?"

Sonny stuttered. "Ah . . . ah . . . my best friend has been expecting his longtime pen pal, Jan, to arrive here. That's all I've heard about this last week. Jan's so beautiful. Jan's so wealthy. She has her own car. He wants to marry Jan," he rambled. "I just got confused."

I took a hard look at Sonny. Was he trustworthy? I recalled a part I'd memorized for a Shakespearean play in high school: "He doth overly much protest." I diverted Sonny's attention back to the map we were perusing.

"Would you like to go up to the Banaue Rice Terraces? Just a few hours north of there?" His brown, manicured finger pointed to a spot on the map.

I placed my finger over the province of Nueva Ecija. "This seems more what I'd like to see."

"There are a few interesting places to visit near Cabanataun City." Sonny looked almost gleeful. "You could travel there and take some side trips."

"I'd like to do that. I got a letter once from someone in Cah . . . bah . . . that place you just mentioned. I might look her up." He didn't need to know that "looking her up" was my prime purpose for being here. "Could I go tomorrow do you think?" I was anxious to start, to do something constructive. "Tell me how to catch the bus that will take me north."

"You would have to take a jeepney to Cubao from here. Then on the corner of New York and Edsa, you'll find the Victory Bus Company station."

My brows knitted in confusion. What was a "jeepney"? Where was "Coo-bow"?

"Can I take a taxi from here to the bus station?" In my mind I imagined a clean, well-marked bus station, looking much like the Trailways or Greyhound Bus stations I knew. I unfolded the city map to plan my strategy.

I peered at the minute streets crammed into the map like cyclone fencing. Cubao seemed undefined on the map. Sonny couldn't understand my fear of facing this huge, unknown, and crowded city.

"I know. I'll go with you to the bus. That way you won't get lost," he suggested.

I sighed in relief. "Thank you so much, Sonny. Could I get a bus schedule, so I'll know when to leave?"

He chuckled. "We don't have bus schedules. I think those buses leave every hour or so. You just go there, and there is always room on a bus. I'm sure they even have air-conditioned buses on those long trips."

"That would be really nice. Could you take me about nine o'clock tomorrow morning?" *For a tourist agent, he sure doesn't seem to know too much about transportation here. Or maybe transportation, like traffic, is also haphazard*—a fact I was to find to be all too true.

"Thank you so much for your help." I waved goodbye as he jauntily walked across the lobby and out the front doors. He seemed in a good mood. I was too. Something niggled at the edge of my mind. Why would a stranger be so helpful to me? I really liked Sonny. He seemed to have an honest personality and was such a friendly soul. Did he have a family, wife, and children? I'd just been thinking about my own needs, not knowing if I had interrupted his plans.

Checking out of this hotel in the morning would solve my cash flow problem. I could probably find a cheaper place to stay in Cabanatuan. My heart felt light . . . relieved.

Sleepy by 8:00 p.m., I went to bed. Anticipation of the unknown tomorrow only filled my mind for a few minutes. I again thanked God who provided a person to guide me in this next step of my trip. I was now beginning my adventure.

EIGHT

Stalemate

Bus Ride to Cabanatuan, July 1980

Without high expectations, breakfast the next day wasn't so disappointing. I enjoyed mango again, plus a sweet roll and coffee. Soon I saw my self-appointed tourist guide come in, looking around to locate where I was sitting. He wore gray slacks and what looked like a new, striped T-shirt. I felt he had dressed up especially for me so I would not be embarrassed to be seen with him. When he spotted me, he hurried over to my table. I offered to order coffee for him, but he declined.

My one bag was packed, and I soon checked out. Sonny reappeared, saying the bus was due to leave at 10:00 a.m. I was happily surprised to hear that Sonny was willing to ride the bus north with me.

"Don't you have to go to work?" I asked.

"I took a couple of days off to show you the Philippines. I just checked in with my boss. I told him you needed me to accompany you to Nueva Ecija. I said I'd be back in a few days," Sonny assured me.

I was flattered, but still puzzled that Sonny would do this. I wondered how much this would cost me. And yet, I was still pleased and grateful I didn't have to travel alone all that way.

After an hour's hectic taxi ride, we arrived at the busy bus station. Families stood together, some people sat on their luggage, and others crowded the available benches. The first aroma that hit my nostrils was the acrid smell of urine from the public bathrooms nearby. I skirted away from the repelling odor, looking for the ticket window. Sonny knew his way around, and people parted to watch us go through to the destinations window: SAN JOSE, NUEVA VISCAYA, ISABELLA, CAGAYAN.

What a relief to finally board the cool bus! What luxury! It had comfortable seats that could even recline. Sonny put my bag in the rack overhead, while I clutched my purse and camera. He was only carrying a small blue bag, which he shoved under the seat ahead of us. I relaxed and sighed contentedly. Sonny seemed puzzled by my action.

"I'm just glad I'm finally on this bus. I don't really enjoy being packed among so many people. The kids—" I didn't want to seem critical of his country, so I cut off my remark about the undisciplined little children running and screaming in the bus depot, demanding some more candy, or Chippies, or the ever-present baby bottle that mom had in her bag.

The relaxation was only temporary. The bus veered recklessly into the helter-skelter traffic. I clutched my seat in fright.

Sonny patted my arm. "You must not be afraid. He knows how to drive."

"This traffic really scares me." I closed my eyes at what seemed another near miss. Give me the orderly traffic in the US any day. Finally, my nerves settled down, and soon I didn't notice the close calls. Instead I watched the people-packed vehicles outside my window.

I turned to Sonny. "Do you have a family?"

"I'm the fifth child in a very poor family. They paid my way through Provincial High School. Then Uncle Oscar, who had a job working in the cane fields in Hawaii, sent me money to pay my college expenses."

I was finding it pleasant to be with Sonny—a strange name for a Filipino man. But he did have a pleasing, sunny personality.

"I studied at FEU, then later at UE," he said.

I must have looked puzzled. I couldn't imagine what the initials meant, but presumed the U stood for university. I was beginning to understand Sonny's accented English.

"Are you married?" Sonny asked me out of the blue.

"My husband died several years ago, and then my mother died." I felt reluctant to tell him about Dad being in the service in the Philippines. Eventually though, with his skillful and sympathetic questioning, I did tell him of Dad's disappearance and the letter years later.

"That's why I'm anxious to visit Cabanatuan. Maybe I can ask at the town hall to see if they have any information about an American living there about 1949 or 1950. I suspect he married a Filipina woman and just stayed here."

"Did your dad ever write about the Japanese?" Sonny asked.

"Not that I can recall. Maybe he wasn't allowed to say much in his letters."

"Was your dad here when the Japanese surrendered?"

"I don't really know. I wasn't born when he left, and I was only a baby when he disappeared. He wrote to my mother for only a couple of years. I can't recall . . . Wait a minute. I remember now. He disappeared just about that time I believe. It was in October 1945."

"Where was your dad stationed?"

"Some place near Gapan. The embassy said it was Camp Palayan. Is that camp still around there?"

"Can I see your dad's letters? Maybe I can help you find where it was."

"I don't have them." I gulped back my tears. "Someone stole all the information I had from my room at the hotel."

"Did you report the theft to the hotel management?"

"Of course, but there seemed to be nothing they could do about it. Either that or they didn't care." I shrugged.

As we drove through a clogged intersection, the bus stopped to let a couple step down.

Sonny said, "This is Gapan. Maybe your dad was right here."

I noticed the distinctive monument right in the middle of the highway, proclaiming this to be Gapan. It was a concrete structure carved with the name of the then mayor who sponsored the landmark.

I rifled through my purse for a hanky. Tears threatened to overflow. *This really could be the same place Dad had been stationed.*

"I didn't mean to make you cry, Sue." He protectively put his hand on my arm. I tried to control a sob, but his sympathy made it all the harder.

"I wish I had known my dad." I sniffled. To hide my moment of weakness, I swallowed and turned to look out at the now green landscape outside the window after passing through Gapan. A fresh, verdant odor of new rain wafted in through the open door when someone else was dropped off a few kilometers further on. I scanned fields and fields of the must luscious green—rice fields.

"This is called the Rice Bowl of the Philippines," Sonny explained. "Rice is grown in this whole area between the eastern Sierra Madre range to the right and Tarlac on the west."

I watched jeepneys of every size, color, and description carrying people to market or work, or even I supposed, on pleasure trips.

"There don't seem to be many cars. Don't people have their own cars?" I asked.

"Most people can't afford cars. These jeepneys are rebuilt from wartime Jeeps. The vehicles can carry from sixteen to twenty people who ride for only a few pesos each. They travel every few minutes to many locations, and they'll stop for you anywhere. Very convenient, don't you think."

That wasn't my first thought. *How inconvenient to sit crammed in there, sitting sideways in the back of an elongated Jeep, not being able to see much but the gutter beside the road and the faces and knees of the person across from you.*

Sonny interrupted my reverie.

"Let's get down in a few minutes. There is a good hotel right on the highway here."

He pulled down my bag from overhead and signaled with a rap on the ceiling to indicate our desire to get off. Pushing through or stepping over a trussed piglet, a live chicken, and numerous tied bundles in the aisles, we inched our way forward to the exit. People had to refold their jump seats in the center aisle and stand up to let us pass, slowing our progress. I shuddered to think what chaos would occur in a serious accident. No aisles free enough to escape through.

We then stepped down, leaving the air-conditioned comfort into the blazing heat of the central plains of Cabanatuan City.

When we walked in from outside, the hotel seemed not much cooler. Two people talked behind the desk, apparently unconcerned with customers. They chatted while we waited.

Sonny interrupted, speaking rapidly in Tagalog. I signed the register and paid 150 pesos for the room. That was only $37.50 in US currency, I calculated.

"Only one room?" a clerk asked. I nodded naively. We got some strange knowing looks. Reluctantly, I left my passport at the desk, and after accepting the key, I was escorted up to my room. Sonny said he would inquire in town to see who might have known Joe de Cou thirty years ago. Before he stepped back into the heat, we arranged to meet at the coffee shop in an hour. I was exhausted from the crowded bus ride, the heat, the sweat, the smells, and the noisy traffic.

I found my room a bare, unwelcoming space compared to The Manila Hotel. The bed was a simple bamboo wood frame with only sparse sheets on a three-inch foam mattress. Bare wires hung from where someone had taken off with the outlet. I looked into the little attached bathroom. There was no shower curtain, no toilet seat or paper, and no free soap, but when I turned on the tap, there was water.

I reassured myself that the price was right and definitely more within my budget than my former luxurious room. The bellboy, who carried my bag, turned on the air conditioner. It was stifling with heat and high humidity. Even after twenty minutes, the air-conditioner did little to cool the room and was extremely noisy.

I was tired, hungry, and annoyed. A quick cold shower felt so refreshing. I laid on the bed and snoozed briefly.

When I was rested, I went downstairs and waited forty-five minutes for Sonny. Finally, I inquired at the desk about his whereabouts.

"He left," a clerk said.

It had been more than an hour. *What a jerk!*

In the coffee shop, I ate a passable meal of rice and *adobo* and went back to my room. Someone had turned off my air conditioner. I turned it on again and my room cooled down as I slept.

When I awoke, I decided my first stop should be at city hall. That's usually where they kept birth and death records. Sonny still was nowhere to be found. I rode in a tricycle—a motorcycle with a sidecar—over to the city hall. I asked for help, wondering why the place looked so temporary. A shrug was the only response I got. I'm sure my English was not that difficult to understand. I asked another person, only to find out that the original city hall had burned down in June this year.

"Would there be any other records of birth, deaths, or marriages in Cabanatuan?" I inquired. I got another shrug and shake of the head.

I left feeling very discouraged. Every step seemed to be blocked in my search for information about my dad.

NINE

In Cabanatuan

Cabanatuan, July 1980

After the disappointment and failure to find information at the city hall, I wandered out into the tropical heat, noise, and confusion. Near the public market I saw what seemed to be a cool place. I entered a small café called Arcegas to buy something to eat before returning to the Manrio Hotel. Sitting down to a hot-dog sandwich and bottle of Coca-Cola, I knew I had to do some serious thinking and planning.

Some Americans came in and smiled at me as they ordered cold drinks. I was the only other American in the place. They came over and asked if I was with the Peace Corps. I shook my head no, but I couldn't shake off the gloom I felt.

"Are you just touring this area, then?" one woman asked.

"Well . . ." I didn't know what to say or how much to tell. "I came up to Cabanatuan to see if my dad who was missing in action here in 1944 might . . . might have his death registered here. But the records were all lost in the burning of the city hall this year. I even wonder if he might have married a girl here and stayed."

"What makes you think that might have happened?" the woman asked sympathetically.

"My mother got a letter many years after dad's disappearance from an Estelle de Cou; de Cou is my maiden name." Well, the sordid details were out. I could talk about it. They didn't seem shocked.

"What did Estelle say in her letter?"

"She really didn't say much. The letter was addressed to my mom. Estelle said she loved Joe and that he meant a lot to her. The only address she gave was Cabanatuan. She wanted to write to Mom. She said something about Joe almost dying in the jungle. He was too sick to walk."

"Did the letter say where he was?" she asked.

"Nothing was very clear, and now the letter has been stolen from my hotel room in Manila." My voice broke. "All the information I needed was also taken." I gulped back tears.

The woman leaned toward me. "What else did the letter say that might give us some information to help you?"

"I remembered it was mailed from here. The postmark wasn't clear, but I recall a 'C' and a 'tuan.' The province was Nueva Ecija. I've got nowhere else to . . . to . . ." I couldn't finish my thought.

"Do you recall any other little details that might help us?" the man asked.

I thought a while, trying to recall the letter, which I'd read so many times. It hadn't been long and was written in simple English. "I believe she said she wanted to go to college. Some sort of initials 'C' then 'L,' I believe. The last letter was 'U.'

"That must be CLSU, which stands for Central Luzon State University. That's right up where we live. Maybe you, or we, could look in their records. Did you notice what year the letter was sent?"

"Yes, it was March 1958. I never even knew about the letter until recently. My mother didn't tell me about it. I only found it among her stuff after her death."

"Would you like to come and stay with us? We'll take you over to CLSU tomorrow to look in their records."

I felt reluctant to take them up on their generosity. But . . .

"I'm Lester and this is Pearl, my wife. We are the Davinses. We're missionaries with the Baptist church and live in Muñoz where the university is. We'd love to have you stay with us."

I brightened. If this couple had been sent by God, this seemed to be the only positive opportunity that had come to me recently. Sonny had left. The rat! All those glowing promises and kind words, then he'd just taken off. I was ticked off at him.

"Okay, I would really appreciate your help," I answered.

"We'd love to help you . . . ah . . ." Lester added.

"I'm Sue Gibson from Powell, Wyoming. I believe God put me and you in this place together." I choked up again.

"We're about ready to drive home. Would you be free to ride with us in our car?"

"Yes, thank you!" I gasped. I had a hard time preventing my relief from showing. "Yes, I'll need to check out of the Manrio Hotel though."

"We'll drive you by there. It's on our way," Pearl said.

I smiled widely. The burning of the city hall wasn't the end of my journey! Finally, there might be another piece to this puzzle to solve. I paid for my food, and when the couple drove me to the hotel, I retrieved my passport and my bag from my room, then met with them a few minutes later.

As we drove north, I related the events that preceded my trip to the Philippines. God was still in charge of me and also of this dubious search. I felt a little more encouraged.

"This stretch of highway north and south always reminds me of a trip we once took, hoping to reach the coast from here." Lester pointed to the right. That was the first time I'd seen dense forest—almost impenetrable in fact. I was glad to be riding in this four-wheel-drive Chevy, but even with it, the road was challenging at times.

"But where does the road lead to eventually?" I asked.

"To the coastal town of Baler in the province of Aurora. That day we drove four hours on that road to only cover twenty miles. The roadbed was washed out in places, the trees nearly met overhead, and I heard monkeys squawking in the trees. I also caught glimpses of the colorful macaws, a type of tropical parrot, in the dense undergrowth."

"Sounds scary," I said. "All I see here is tranquil green rice fields as far as the eye can see. It's hard to believe primeval forest could be that close. Why would anyone want to build a road into this Amazon-like jungle?"

"When we ventured through there," Pearl said, "we found a rest house, halfway to the coast. We learned that this road was constructed because a past president of the Philippines, Manuel Quezon, was from the coastal town of Baler and wanted access other than the risky outrigger canoe trip on the open Pacific Ocean."

Lester laughed. "I suppose in Quezon's day, the president's means of transportation was usually horse and buggy. I recall going through a museum in Baler and seeing a 1937 Chrysler on display, which he had owned. Maybe he demanded access so he could drive home in style and show off his car. Who knows? That was a long time ago—about the time I was born."

My body jerked back and forth at the close misses along the way—a stray dog across the road, undisciplined traffic, even people walking on the road bank. It wasn't an easy drive, but Lester Davins managed quite well and pointed out landmarks along the way.

"Looks like a squall is coming on," Pearl said.

"Not a problem. We'll be home soon," Lester commented, staring up at the lowering rain clouds.

Lester continued his travelogue. "The Japanese were said to have hastily hidden their confiscated treasure somewhere up there." He gestured to the right and shrugged. "Who knows? It's fun to speculate though, and many have tried to find it."

TEN

Muñoz

Muñoz, July 1980

The heaviness in the air soon turned into a full-fledged downpour. The wipers' valiant effort could barely make the road visible, and I wondered how Lester could drive at all. There were sections where the road became a stream, but vehicles still managed to pass through it, throwing up sheets of water to each side. Even though we were protected in the vehicle, I felt encased in steam. All the windows were closed and fogging up. I cracked a window and got a face full of water. Big mistake!

I noticed children and even teenagers making the most of a free shower as water poured off metal roofing. With a sliver of soap, a gleeful grin, and minimal clothing, the rain became a celebration of cleanliness. Oh to be young again and enjoy the simple pleasures of life! It made me want to join their fun.

"It's rain like this that grows such abundant rice here," Lester commented.

Finally, the heavy rain abated a little, and we arrived at their home. Dusk turned rapidly into night, so typical of the tropics. It was only six o'clock. No long summer twilights like I was used to in Powell.

We entered a side door that led to an open area with concrete floors. It included no furniture, only some crates and boxes, not really a very appealing entrance to a home. Then I saw the majestic stairway, which led us upstairs to the main living area, I presumed. The staircase was ten feet wide, with carved banisters, a work of art themselves. Never before had I seen such delicate and lovely old woodwork. I touched the satin-smooth wood and oohed and ahhed in appreciation. In the light of the next day, I noticed each step was a slightly different hue of mahogany wood.

Upstairs, the stately rooms with their mahogany walls rose up to the delicately carved panels under the fifteen-foot ceiling. These carvings stood out against the white-painted ceilings. I thought they must be mahogany wood paneling, but these were solid wood walls, an inch thick, and were constructed of one piece of wood from floor to ceiling.

As I gaped in amazement, Pearl said, "We were told this is one of the few houses to remain standing after the war. The rest of the town was burned to the ground."

I remembered one of Dad's letters that told about towns being completely destroyed. I wish I had his letters to refer to again. I came out of my reminiscences to hear her continue.

"This highway was the only north and south access route. A lot of the fighting occurred here as the Japanese fled north, followed closely by the pursuing American/Filipino troops."

She waved her arm vaguely at the road we had just turned off, which ran directly in front of the gate to this compound. Later I was to learn their house had been the Japanese officers' quarters during their occupation time. The enlisted men billeted in the grade school across the street. The younger Davins children had attended that very school recently.

Early the next morning, I explored the outside of the lovely old house. It had unpainted, weather-beaten siding, but was adorned with subtle carvings adhering to the mahogany-paneled outer walls. This was the kind of Spanish structure you'd expect to find with gargoyles at the corners of each eave, the precursor to downspouts.

Looking around the large enclosed yard, I was inspired by the colorful orchids attached to coconut palms, also papaya, banana, acacia, and mango trees. I was amused that the goats had trimmed all the mango trees to goat height. An interesting place!

Then a shiver went through me as I stood where the action had taken place during the time my dad was in this area. *How many of the enemy my dad fought had actually lived in this old house, under this very roof?* I'm not the kind of person who feels that places have an aura, but shivers went up my arms and down my spine thinking about the past.

"I find it fascinating to live in a house with a lot of history," Lester commented at my elbow. "This corner of our living room was damaged by an American plane that was shot down. It's been fixed, of course, but it's interesting nonetheless."

He turned to me. "Sue, I remember talking with an old friend of mine, Bartholome, from Villa Santos. He was here when the Japanese forces fled north through this town. Bartholome is an old man now. He was just a kid at the end of the war and curious. He saw the smoke rising from the town of Muñoz, so the next day he walked the few miles to see what had happened."

I listened closely, hoping Lester's stories would give me a hint as to where to search for what happened to my dad.

"I saw that all the trees were burned," he told me, "and only three or four houses were still standing." This house was spared from the fires, even as smoke still rose from all the ruins.

"It was awful," my friend said. "He didn't know where everyone had escaped to. Forty-five or so Japanese tanks were put out of commission clear up the valley between Muñoz and Santo Thomas and San Jose. He said he and his friends climbed up on these huge tanks and played war for weeks until the army came to drag them away."

"What an interesting story," I interjected. "I wonder if my dad was a part of the army doing the chasing that day?"

Lester Davins looked sympathetic, but only shrugged his shoulders.

"Sue, Bartholome is special to me for another reason—his hands," Lester said.

"What about his hands?" I asked.

"I traveled to Villa Santos for a Bible study every week, and one time, Bartholome approached me. 'I'm a useless old man,' he said, sighing. He showed me his ugly misshapen hands. 'I can't hold a rope any longer. I used to take the *carabao* [water buffalo] out to pasture, but now I can't close a fist to hold a rope. I'm of no help to my family anymore!' He was a broken man."

Lester continued his story. "I took his misshapen hands in mine, bowed my head, and I asked God for the ability to say this in Ilocano. I prayed, 'Lord, this man needs your power and strength to open and close his hands. Please restore him! Thank you.' I'm sure God understood my ineptness in his language and knew what I meant to say."

Lester continued. "The next time I saw Bartholome, he greeted me in triumph, opening and closing his hands to show what God had done. That answer to my prayer was a real boost to *my* faith, the faith of that farmer's family, and even the whole barrio."

"Amazing!" I said. "Is that why you're still a missionary here?"

"Of course! At least one of the reasons."

Turning back to the yard, I pointed and said, "I can't remember what that luxuriant plant is called that's growing over the wall there."

Lester let out a loud chortle. "That's a split-leaf philodendron. I just about got fired from a job several years ago due to that plant." My eyebrows rose in puzzlement.

Lester continued his explanation. "While a seminarian back home, I worked as the church janitor and left the social hall's precious split-leaf philodendron too close to the plate-glass window one winter day. It nearly froze."

"Oops," I said.

"The women in the WMS—the Women's Missionary Society—had a fit, but luckily the plant survived and so did I." We both laughed.

"A year later when we arrived in the Philippines, I saw a water buffalo munching on an abundant split-leaf philodendron growing over a wall. I laughed and said, 'Chomp away. Live dangerously!'"

ELEVEN

At The Pool

Muñoz, July 1980

The Davinses and I discussed our plans for the day over a huge breakfast of homemade hotcakes and syrup flavored with calamansi.

"This is calamansi," Pearl explained, holding up a wee citrus fruit similar to a lime. "It's our approach to lemons—a great flavor but tedious to squeeze because they are so small."

Later, with good food in my stomach, the future seemed optimistic, and I was ready to push forward.

Lester asked, "Would you be interested in a swim? I usually swim early each morning. Pearl, do you have time for a swim this morning?"

Pearl shook her head no. "I have six loaves of bread rising. I'd love to, but maybe another day."

My immediate thought this July morning was that I hoped the pool was heated. But then I realized that in this heat, the sun probably did a good job of warming up the water. I never seemed to be free of perspiration at any time of the day or night.

"I would really enjoy that. Does it cost much?"

71

"Won't cost you anything," Lester said. "My children attend school at the university, so we can swim anytime with very little monthly cost. You'll be my guest."

Lester rapped on a door off the living room. "Son, want to go for a swim before school today?"

"Yeah, I'll be right out, Dad. That would be great." Within a few minutes, Larry appeared with a large backpack full of books.

After leaving Pearl to her bread baking, we drove the mile to the university to swim. Once I slipped into the cool water of the pool, I closed my eyes in pleasure. *What a luxury!* I swam a few lengths as Lester talked to someone at the pool's edge. Then he called me over to introduce me to an elderly Filipino gentleman resting at the side of the pool.

"Leon, this is Sue Gibson, a visitor of ours from Powell, Wyoming."

"Good to meet you, Sue. What brings you to Muñoz?" he asked. I was amazed at his fluency in English.

Lester must have seen the surprise on my face and explained, "You may wonder at Leon's English. He's lived many years in various parts of the US and has returned here for retirement."

"I did wonder, I must admit," and then I looked at Leon. "Actually, I'm on a quest to find my long-lost dad."

"Why is that? I've heard of dads losing their daughters, but never a daughter losing a dad!" he said with humor in his voice.

"I never knew my dad because he was stationed here with the US Army when I was born. He was declared missing in action about 1945 and was last seen up here somewhere."

"What makes you think . . . what motivates you to come and look for him so long after the fact?" Leon inquired.

Lazily kicking my legs in the water, I wondered how much to tell him. "I went through my mother's papers after her death last year. There was a letter, also notes from a phone call, after his plane went down. He was presumed dead in the mountains east of Cabanatuan."

"Sounds like a fascinating mystery!"

"In some ways, I'm reluctant to discover what I think might have happened. All the correspondence from my dad was warm and loving and with great expectations of reuniting after the war. But this letter I found dated in 1958 was from a woman, Estelle de Cou. That was my maiden name. So all I could imagine was that . . ." My voice faltered, and my eyes teared up. I dreaded putting into words the feelings of my heart.

"You know, Sue, your saying that reminds me of a student I met here in the pool in about 1955, I believe. What got my attention was her astonishing grasp of English. She switched to English when she realized her backwoods Ilocano accent from Gabaldon did not communicate too well. I asked her how she had learned such great English, colloquially and grammatically correct. She had an interesting story to tell.

"She told me, 'I learned it from an American serviceman whom my family had helped. Well, actually, my dad rescued him from certain death in the jungle. This man became my teacher. He spent all his time teaching me English, and we, in turn, taught him to speak Ilocano.'"

Leon continued. "I remember that conversation clearly. She had only good things to say about this man who was recuperating in their home for an extended period of time, I surmised. She lived in a remote area—a *kaingin*, really. Let me see what you would call that in English." He paused. "Basically, a small hut in slash-and-burn agriculture. She said they had to hike five days out to a road. Her English teacher never regained enough strength to make that trip out to what we call civilization. I remember it as a sad story. She was a lovely girl."

He paused and then perked up again. "Oh, I remember another aspect about Essie—that was her name. Once she came to my house to see if I could exchange a US bill for pesos. There were no banks in Muñoz then. I hadn't seen US currency for years. I had to verify its genuineness at a bank in Cabanatuan where I exchanged it. Essie was an amazing person—poised and confident. I came to like her a lot after my few contacts with her. She seemed determined to get a college education, though she really had little or no money to do so. She worked as a maid for the Supremos, a family in town. You could ask them about her."

"Thank you for telling me about her, Leon," I said.

"I hope it helps."

I wondered if there was anything to Leon's story. At least it was a lead to a serviceman who had been in this area, or at least near Cabanatuan. I closed my eyes as I swam another length, thanking God for leading me to this man.

"May we go and talk to the Supremos some time?" I asked Lester as we drove home. I was still dripping wet, but pleasantly cooled after the swim.

"Don't expect a warm welcome from Mrs. Supremo," Lester answered. "The wealthy people of Spanish descent are prone to be quite uppity, proud of their own wealth and position in the community. These owners of huge tracts of land, mostly rice farms and mills, were able to remain on the land by buying off the Japanese invaders with Spanish antique carvings they had acquired in Europe. They bargained with their gold-encrusted idols as collateral, thus remaining in their large homes. They continued to mill the rice, then sold it to the invading army and the population in general."

"But what if the poor farmers themselves couldn't afford to buy, or eat, the rice they had raised themselves?" I asked.

"They would hold back some for their families. I've seen large mortar-and-pestle wood forms, which take two in harmonious rhythm to pound the husks off the rice manually," Lester said. "A tedious process, but it gets the job done cheaply."

We drove in silence for a while. "Well," he said, "about going to see Mrs. Supremo in your search for answers. I have to conduct a wedding at 4:00 a.m. tomorrow morning out in the barrios—the villages nearby. But we could visit her after that. How does that sound?"

"Great!" Now I needed to think of questions to ask the Supremo family.

TWELVE

Secret Diggings

Palayan, July 1980

*I*t *didn't make any sense to stay with Sue,* Sonny thought. *It was obvious she didn't know anything.* So he left her at the hotel and followed up on a lead in that last letter from Joe de Cou, leaving for Palayan. Waving down a jeepney, he headed east out of Cabanatuan toward the former army base near Palayan.

Farmers in the area seldom moved from the land they owned. Sonny thought it should be fairly easy to ask around about that farmer who fed his pigs from US Army slops.

Where would a bare-existence farmer get earrings to sell like those described in his letter, except from the hidden wealth the Japanese were trying to hide?

Sonny stepped down from his transportation vehicle at a simple little store. He ordered one cold Coca-Cola and looked around for a likely prospect to interrogate. He didn't see anyone who might be in the know. They were all too young. He took his drink over to a rough bench under a mango tree where two old men sat passing the time of day as they stared at passersby.

"Are you one of those Army guys over there?" one of them asked, gesturing with his lips and chin toward the high fence. Sonny pretended to not understand Ilocano, so he asked, *"Paki-ulit sa Tagalog*! [Please repeat that in Tagalog!]."

The men laughed, then said to each other, "This kid must be one of those young men who pretend to be soldiers, but spend all night moving earth around behind that high fence with bright lights. They spend every night laughing, singing, and swearing as they work. They come out filthy each morning to laze around their camp, sleeping, doing nothing, saying nothing. They aren't very friendly. Won't talk to us."

Then switching into the Tagalog language, one of the old men turned to Sonny. "What do you do every night behind that fence? Digging for treasure?" They laughed as though this was a big joke.

Sonny shrugged. "I'm not part of them. I just came over from Cabanatuan. Have you men lived here for many years? Where is the army camp?"

These old men seemed to think this amusing too. "You are right now in what used to be the camp. We were stationed here too—worked right along with the American army—and we even speak Ingles!"

"My father was stationed here," Sonny said, concocting a story on the spot, "and he talked a lot about working in the mess hall for the army. He even said that the farmers in this area had very fat pigs, because he took out their scraps, peelings, and leftovers to give to the farmers."

Another chortle erupted from these old men who had little to amuse themselves these days except speculation about the goings-on of outsiders. They looked at each other. "Eh, Miguel, you recall anyone who had a piggery back then?"

"No. As I recall, the Japanese systematically stole the pigs. Wise farmers took them farther into the forest where the Japanese were usually too superstitious to go."

"What was your dad's name? Maybe we knew him?" one old man asked.

Sonny made up a fictitious name that didn't remind them of anyone they recalled. He stood up. "I think I'll go over and watch what these military men are doing. I'm curious."

One old codger stood up, too, surprisingly spry for his wrinkled appearance. Grabbing the back of Sonny's T-shirt, he sputtered, "I wouldn't if you value your life. They are really mean. Killed a little kid who dug under the fence last week who only wanted to watch what was going on."

"Police did nothing about it either," the other man added.

Sonny knew from Cesar that "The Task Force Restoration" begun in recent years was not really to discourage insurgency but to secretly excavate treasure for President Marcos. One rumor had come to Sonny's attention that this army contingent had been digging out near this camp every night for several months.

Sonny spent several days moving around the town and talking to various people, any who were willing to talk. They seemed to be intimidated by the strong military presence. There were threats made when questions were asked, and the army helicopters came every week. He heard that two Huey military-type helicopters had escorted a presidential chopper that ferried President Marcos to the site one early morning.

When Sonny was accosted by an armed soldier questioning his motives for hanging around, he was afraid the same thing would happen to him as it had to that kid.

He decided to quit and go home. He sat down on a rock in the shade of a large mango tree beside the road after walking for a while. *Wonder what else I can do to get information?* Then Sonny remembered the ancient letters from Joe that were still in his bag. The letters were all he had left to help him discover where the Japanese might have hidden, in a hurry, that immense amount of wealth.

Opening the packet, Sonny picked a letter at random. He'd forgotten that these letters were not in a language he understood readily. He read, "Who do you have mowing your lawn now that you don't have me there?" Sonny wrinkled his brow. What did that mean, "mow your lawn?" He laid the page on the rock beside him. It fluttered off in the slight breeze, landing in the stream nearby. He watched the page of graying paper float away slowly.

I don't care. That letter won't be of much help to me.

Opening another month's letter, he read, "I remember pulling the quilt up to our ears and snuggling in to forget it was twenty degrees outside."

More puzzling words. He threw that page into the water, along with several others. Watching them float away, he thought they would make nice pieces of paper for some farmer's wife to retrieve downstream to light her breakfast fire.

As Sonny waited for an available ride, he delighted in setting sail the accumulation of love notes from an absent lover and dad of so many years ago. The very letters that Sue would have cherished into her old age had now set sail to become lodged in some mud bank or culvert.

Sonny let several vehicles pass, too full to accommodate one more clinger-on. When he arrived at Cabanatuan, he enquired at the Manrio Hotel for Sue. With no explanation, she had checked out the same day they had both checked in. "So your *querida* stood you up, did she?" the desk clerk taunted.

THIRTEEN

Inquiries at the University

Muñoz, July 1980

Lester returned from his 4:00 a.m. wedding about five hours later that morning. Pearl and I were sitting on the sofa chatting.

"I've never heard of weddings at that hour of the morning," I commented when he arrived.

"Actually, barrio weddings are similar to weddings in biblical times. It involves a big, whole-town celebration that lasts all day and all night, sometimes longer." I shook my head in disbelief as he continued. "I often leave before the feasting, but today I couldn't run out so easily. I have a vested interest in this couple, so I had some coffee and *puto*—the white, steamed cake—at the breakfast.

"I've watched Fe and Lito's courtship from the beginning. They came to the first group Bible study. There is no dating here—just meaningful looks in the living room, maybe meeting out in the fields as they work, then singing in church, helping with the younger kids in their class. That sort of courtship. So after the wedding is really the first time they will be alone together.

"Pearl, do you remember talking with Basilio that day we were taking him to his wedding?"

"You mean about his really needing to shave before his wedding?" Pearl giggled.

"Yeah, he had used the only razor blade he had in his simple home," he said, "to shave the pig that day in preparation for the famous *Lechon,* or roast pig, for the wedding feast."

They both laughed, and I couldn't help but join them.

"Basilio had little or no beard," Lester said, "but not being clean-shaven for his own wedding! He would have been mortified. I believe a friend finally found a razor blade to help him out."

I laughed at the image of the poor young man and his predicament.

"Enough talk about weddings," Lester said, looking at me. "I'm dead on my feet. Do you mind if I shower first before going over to the Supremos? Mrs. Supremo might be rather disappointed if Father Billings arrives looking this unkempt."

"Why would she call you Father Billings?" I asked.

"All clergy, in the tradition of most Roman Catholics, are priests and thus called Father out of respect. I don't bother to correct them. After all, I am actually a father and a priest in the biblical sense." Lester chuckled.

After Lester freshened up, we drove west over non-paved roads with no sidewalks. I didn't see any lawns either, but there were a lot of carefully swept dirt areas around homes built of bamboo-woven sides raised off the ground by three- or four-foot stilts.

"Why are these houses built so high off the ground?" I asked. "Does it flood here?"

"Yes. You noticed the sudden and intense rain we had yesterday."

I nodded. "It came down in buckets."

"These very poor people have to protect their belongings from flood waters, especially their sacks of rice. Also, often their pigs, water buffalo, and chickens seek shelter under the house during storms. That area can be closed off.

"But truthfully, often these huts are no shelter at all. A typhoon can sweep through, blowing off their corrugated tin roofing, collapsing the whole structure and endangering the lives of those cringing inside. During each typhoon, we often have all the neighbors seeking shelter in our sturdy home. They come with a few bundles of blankets and clothes, sacks of rice, and often with a prizefighting cock or pigs."

"Then what do you do with all this sudden company," I said in amazement. "Throw a party?"

"That's exactly what happens," Lester said. "When the electricity goes off, we turn on our big gas lamp, then get out the Monopoly board and also play card games. Helps cut down the tension. The women and children shelter with us, and the men, including myself, run back and forth trying to save more stuff from their homes that have been knocked down by the high winds. Everyone is wet, chilled, tired, and hungry. Pearl will usually cook up a huge pot of rice and soup made from a drowned chicken and any available vegetables."

Soon, my thoughts of the poor people who had to suffer through typhoons faded away. Ahead of us, I noticed a lovely landscaped yard and a concrete-block home behind high walls as we approached. *This must be where we're headed.*

After Lester parked, we got out of the car, walked up to the fancy double doors, and he rapped the knocker on the large wood doors.

"Yes," a woman said in a cool voice as she unlocked the door. "Well, Father Billings, why have you come to my house today?"

We waited to be asked inside.

"Could we get some information from you, Ma'am?"

"Anything, Father. Please come inside." We sat on an elegant, but uncomfortable, settee in her *sala*. She seated herself in a large, fan-shaped chair across from us.

"What is it you want to know?" Mrs. Supremo asked.

"We want to ask you about a girl who worked for you many years ago," Lester started. "Her name was Essie, a girl who was attending CLSU. This would be about 1958 or '59."

"I don't recall much about maids. They come and go quickly. Usually, they come in with lies and go out with something of mine in their bags."

"This girl, maybe older than you usually hired, spoke excellent English we are told," Lester spoke for me. He knew the culture and protocol in what seemed to be a hostile interrogation. I was anxious to hear her answers.

Mrs. Supremo seemed to be made of solid marble, similar to her shiny hard floors in the entryway.

"I vaguely remember that girl from Gabaldon, too much of a smart-aleck for her own good. Thought she could talk with me on an equal basis because she could speak English. She was only a country farm girl. I told her to leave when I thought she had stolen some of my jewelry. I don't remember anything else." Mrs. Supremo stood, which was an indication that we should stand and leave too. We did and thanked her for her help, even though we didn't learn much.

On our drive back home, Lester clued me in about wealthy women like Mrs. Supremo, often of Spanish descent, who were prone to treat maids with contempt, even cruelty . . . almost like slaves. They also treated visitors with suspicion, flaunted their wealth, and usually ruled the roost at home. Mrs. Supremo's husband had been dead for a few years. This left her in charge of the vast farms and rice mills. Both her children were now studying in Madrid, he'd heard.

I was pretty depressed about how little I had learned about Essie.

"Let's see what information we can get at the university," Lester said, trying to bolster my spirits a little.

We drove back to the university where we'd been yesterday. When we entered the registrar's office, it seemed to take forever before anyone even acknowledged that we stood at the counter. When their gossip session was over, one woman asked us what we wanted.

"We want to inquire about a former student here," Lester said. "She probably attended school here in 1958 or 1959."

"That information is stored in the boxes stacked in the basement. Write down the name, and I'll have the file clerk look it up in the alphabetical listings. Tell me what her course was too."

She accepted the piece of paper with "Estelle de Cou" written on it.

"You don't know her course?"

"No," I replied.

"Come back next week, and we'll see what we can find."

I wanted immediate answers, but communication and action seemed to progress frustratingly slowly in this country. I glanced at the crowds of students exiting buildings, talking with each other. Few students seemed older than their twenties. I guess older students were rare here. The older people emerging from doors must be instructors, gauging by the respect shown them when a student held the door open for them.

This definitely was not a very satisfactory day. How could I follow up on this girl that Leon Carbonel had talked to? She must have lived someplace besides the Supremos during her time studying here.

"How could we find out where Essie may have lived while here?" I asked Lester.

"Let me ask around. There must be some person who remembers her. I'll try the post office first."

But with only a name from the distant past, no one working at the post office could recall any specific mail recipient with the description we gave them.

What a disappointing day!

FOURTEEN

The Wake

Muñoz, July 1980

I tossed and turned that night, unable to sleep. It seemed as though every step forward was followed by two steps back. Then I recalled the one place I could always get an answer. I set my mind on God and His plan for this trip. Soon I was sound asleep, resting easily in God's lap.

I woke to the most beautiful sunrise on my sixth morning in the Philippines. The acacia trees between here and the Sierra Madre Mountains were silhouetted on the orange and cool-blue sky. I breathed in the refreshing breeze; seventy degrees seemed cool. If I remembered rightly, that was warmer than the temperature I set my thermostat at home during the winters in Wyoming.

I felt a new vigor with the new day. At the desk in my room, I read God's Word and prayed for guidance.

Wandering into the kitchen, I could see the reddish sunrise grow on the green-and-copper Santol tree outside through the window. I asked Pearl what its name meant.

"In English, it would be Custard Apple," she said.

Later I tasted its fruits. They were custard like, only mildly sweet, and had large seeds to spit out once they were divested of their custard-like covering. The Davinses said the fruit was quite constipating, but excellent medication when one was plagued with diarrhea, a common ailment in the tropics I'd discovered.

That day I looked through the notes I'd written down on my journey and examined the information I now had about my dad and Estelle de Cou. I thought of ways I might secure more information about her.

The Davinses had an important training session that day, so I was on my own. I visited their son Larry's piggery. Actually, it consisted of one little pig in an enclosure. He was raising it as a project for school, much like Future Farmers of America in some US schools.

Then I picked a basket of lima beans growing up the enclosing walls of the house. They were better than any canned limas I'd ever eaten. We ate them for lunch, sautéed with pork, garlic, and onions and served with rice.

In the afternoon, I laid down and took a siesta because of the heat since it seemed everyone else did too.

After supper as the family and I lingered at the table, I heard the strains of a band playing "Bridge over Troubled Waters." "Is there a party going on down the street?" I asked.

The reply came from Larry, the Davinses' sixteen-year-old son. "No, my friend Marlon died this week. That's his wake. Dad, can I go down there? Please!"

"Go ahead, son, but be back here before I go to Marlon's house for our meeting. You have homework to do, I presume."

I had a vague idea what a wake was, but I had never been to one. "May I go with you? Is that permitted?" I enquired of the family.

Larry stood up. "Of course! You'll enjoy celebrating his life."

Enjoy? His friend dies, and he can say "enjoy?"

"We'll walk," Larry said. "It's only a short way. The road has already dried from our daily afternoon shower. Simon and Garfunkel are my favorite album too." Larry sang along as we walked toward the brightly lit house.

"In my mind, 'Bridge over Troubled Waters' seemed a rather upbeat song for a wake," I said.

"My dad explained it to me this way," Larry said. "They play the music that would have appealed to the deceased when she or he was alive. Thus, this song appeals to me and did to Marlon too. I often hear 'Santa Claus Is Coming to Town,' at every baby's funeral, or 'I Come to the Garden Alone' for old people."

"I'm curious, Larry. Why did you say I'd 'enjoy' this evening, even though your friend just died?" His answer surprised me.

"A wake is a time to party it up, as if your friend was only going on a long-awaited trip. We play games, gamble, drink . . . uh, everyone else drinks . . . not me," he clarified. "Everyone relates stories of the person's life. They joke and sing along with the band. Later, my dad and mom will come with twenty or thirty people from our church. Once the band has gone home, they'll sing, talk, and Dad will give a sermon on heaven and how to get there."

"But . . ." I interrupted, "aren't the parents and family all devastated?"

Larry shrugged. "Sure, his mom and grandma will probably be weeping by the coffin . . . pretty loud at times. They need the distraction. Marlon's dad and friends will be drinking and also hammering the coffin together in the back."

Rather an unusual approach to the reality of death, but refreshing, nonetheless. If we all thought of death as just going on a long-anticipated luxury cruise, instead of the end of a life here on earth, we'd be better adjusted.

As we approached the family's home, we saw fifty or more people playing games or eating, and some sitting quietly on benches or talking to each other.

I approached cautiously, feeling very much out of place here, but outgoing Larry had no such qualms. In his enthusiasm, he grabbed my hand.

"Let's go talk to Marlon!" Marlon was lying stiff there in the coffin, mind you. It was a little bizarre. "Mar, how's it going? Resting comfortably?"

I cringed.

I sat down on the wooden bench next to the grieving mother, a woman draped all in black, as were most of the people there. Tears filled my eyes too. I felt my own loss again, as if my husband's death had only been this week too.

Marlon's mother placed her hand on my knee, comforting me. She shared, "My best friend in college used to say to me, 'God never places you in a situation where He isn't right there with you.' That friend visited us here last night, and she reminded me of that."

"Thanks," I sputtered. "But at times it's so hard to really . . . apply this truth." *I'd also remembered that same sentiment expressed, but where?*

"Thanks for coming to Marlon's remembrance," his mother said, and then she looked up at others waiting to console her.

I smiled and left, going in search of Larry who was yakking with some friends, but not in English. Somehow, I had come to console this mother, but instead she had consoled me.

Someone put a plate of food in my hands, as well as Larry's. He tucked into that food as though he'd not eaten for a week. I didn't feel like eating at all. Larry leaned close and whispered in my ear, "Just take a bite or two, so you won't hurt their feelings, then put it down. It won't go to waste." I must have given him a horrified look. "Oh, it's not what you think. The pigs will eat it for breakfast tomorrow."

Life here is truly different. Our recycle bin is the pigs' feast here!

FIFTEEN

Wisco's Hardware

Muñoz, 1980

"I'm going downtown and ask questions in Muñoz," I said, as I picked up my bag with some Filipino pesos and a notebook. I tossed the comment over my shoulder to the Davinses who still sat at the breakfast table, discussing their plans.

"Who are you going to talk to?" asked a girl I hadn't noticed in the living room. She looked up from taking notes from the *Encyclopedia Britannica*. "I might have some answers to your questions. I've lived in Muñoz my whole life. I'm Lita Mendoza. The Davinses let me use their resource books for homework assignments."

"Oh, I didn't notice you there. I'm Sue Gibson. I'm going to try to talk to some older folk who would have been in Muñoz twenty-five years ago. It would have to be people your parents' age or older."

"What information are you trying to get?" she persisted.

"I'm trying to find out where a woman who attended CLSU twenty-five years ago might have lived. Her name was Estelle de Cou. I got some information from Leon Carbonell at the swimming pool the other day. He had known a student by the name of 'Essie,' who spoke excellent English. He knew she had worked at the Supremos. We asked there about a maid they hired and fired, but Mrs. Supremo wouldn't say where Essie went after leaving her employ. Both of these students had spoken excellent American English. I've wondered if they could be the same person. Estelle's name didn't show up in the old records at the registrar's office at CLSU. Now the only thing I can think to do is ask questions in town."

"I don't know if this will help," Lita replied. "My dad is a carpenter at CLSU. He purchases all his construction materials at Wisco's Hardware in town. He mentioned several times about a girl who worked there, who spoke excellent English. She was also attending CLSU."

"Would you be willing to take me to see Mr. Wisco, so I can talk with him?"

"I'd be glad to. I've just finished my English assignment. Wisco's Hardware is not too far from where I live in town. I'm sure the owner will be there."

As we stood at the side of the highway directly fronting the Davins's large house, Lita put out a hand and with a loud "pssssst," hailed a means of transportation she called a tricycle. As my mind conjured up the image of a four-year-old gleefully peddling down the highway, a large motorcycle equipped with a sidecar stopped for us. I'm glad I wasn't overweight and Lita was slim; we barely fit in that narrow space. With a refreshing breeze in our faces and the smell of newly harvested rice in our nostrils, we buzzed down the highway into town.

Lita informed the tricycle driver that we'd get off at Wisco's Hardware. Lita and I paid him fifty centavos as we unfolded ourselves from the little vehicle. My mind did a quick money exchange, realizing that was only a few pennies in US currency.

In front of us, the large dingy sign over the fake storefront said, Wisco's Hardware." It was not really a very attractive business. It was dimly lit and crammed from ceiling to floor with everything from parts, nails, hoses, fencing wire, lumber, pig feed, and more. David Wisco, a handsome man in his fifties or sixties, and capable in demeanor, seemed willing to drop everything to help with my questions.

"Sure, I remember Estelle. She worked here for three or four years in the afternoons and evenings. She was going to CLSU in the daytime. She was working full-time while taking twenty credit hours. She was a really bright and honest girl—very determined to finish college. She was taking Business Administration, so her work here improved as she learned. I don't know when she slept. She lived in a little house we provide for our maids and workers, but she stayed up most of the night studying. All she had for light was a kerosene lamp. We really missed her when she graduated and went to Cabanatuan to get a job and live with her aunt and uncle."

"Was she married?" I asked.

"Not that I knew of. She never mentioned a man in her life. She seemed to snub the young men who came in here, who were more eager to talk with her than purchase my hardware." Mr. Wisco laughed.

"What kind of person was she?"

"The kind of employee I would love to have again. I could totally trust her, even when I had to go into Manila to buy supplies. She never took anything, and I never caught her in a lie, which is more than I can say for most of my employees. I was amazed at her mastery of English. She even taught me a few English words I'd not heard. She mentioned once that an American had tutored her when she was young. She didn't share many details. She choked up with tears anytime I asked her about this teacher of hers. I think he must have died just before she came to work for me. Her grief seemed so raw."

"Would you know where she moved to in Cabanatuan, or the name of her aunt and uncle there?" Excited, my words spilled out fast. I was getting closer to answers. I could feel it in my heart."

"Her uncle's name was Andaya. Just a minute and let me see if I have a record that old in my book." He muttered as he thumbed through a worn little address book with yellowed and termite-eaten pages. It was still being used this many years later, and I was amazed he could still read the writing.

"Yes, yes, I have it here under her name: Estrelita B. Gonzales. Andaya Gonzales. I just put down, 'near the Catholic church.' I hope that will help you."

But the names were all wrong. "Was her name Estrelita Gonzales?" I asked. "I thought you said 'Estelle' earlier?"

"She called herself 'Estelle'—a nickname. A habit we have here in the Philippines." David Wisco was truly a likable man and so helpful by giving us his full attention even though customers waited for him. There were so many clues that pointed to the fact that I'd found my Estelle de Cou.

Lita and I thanked him for his help and left the store. I knew I needed to find the Andaya Gonzales family in Cabanatuan soon. I wrote down the names in my notepad before I forgot. I also wrote down her other name—Estrelita. As of now, I had three separate names for the same person, if she was the same person.

"I could go with you to Cabanatuan tomorrow after my morning class," Lita offered. Luckily, I only have one class on Saturday."

"Would you? I feel like that's expecting too much of you," I said. "But I will feel much more confident if I have someone who speaks the language and knows the city."

"Not a problem. I'll come by the Davinses' for you at noon. Can you get home on a tricycle, the same way we did coming into town?"

I nodded. "I think so."

"Good. I only live half a mile down this direction, so I'll leave you now."

"Thank you for helping me," I said.

Lita waved and walked out of sight. The heaviness I'd felt earlier had lifted like a wisp of smoke in the air. I was close to finding out the truth about my dad.

SIXTEEN

Estelle's Aunt

Cabanatuan, The Philippines, July 1980

As I awoke at the Davinses', I listened to the pleasant cheep-cheep-cheep of newborn fighting cocks in the neighbors' pens next door, accompanied by mother hen's deeper cluck-cluck-cluck. Then the raucous crow of the rooster pushed me into full wakefulness. I wrinkled my nose. The odor coming from those chickens was not as pleasant as their wake-up calls.

I turned my attention to God's Word to give me the wisdom I needed to face this day ahead. I opened my Bible to a passage I'd read on one of the first days I was in the Philippines—the event when Abraham's servant had gone to a far country to find a wife for Isaac. He had asked God for an exceptional miracle, praying, "When I'm beside the town well, and girls come out to draw water, may the girl I ask for a drink of water from be the girl you want me to approach. And if she also offers to draw water for my camels, this will be further verification." I reread this amazing story in Genesis, chapter 24. I especially enjoyed the part where it described the man watching her draw countless jars of water for his thirsty caravan of camels.

"Without saying a word, the man watched her closely to learn whether or not the Lord had made his journey success-ful." I wanted this same faith to believe that my journey would be successful too. I wanted to be able to say at the end of today, even as this servant did, "As for me, the Lord has led me on the journey to the house of my master's relatives." In my case, of course, it would be to the house of Estelle de Cou's relatives.

At breakfast, talking to my hosts, I described Lita's and my interview with David Wisco and my desire to go to Cabanat-uan to find the Andaya Gonzales couple. Lester and Pearl were pleased to hear that Lita was willing to go with me.

"I would suggest that you pack your stuff and take your bag with you when you go," Pearl advised. "Sure, it means lugging a little more around with you, but if you find out the information you are looking for, you may not need to come back here."

"We do welcome you to come back though," Pearl contin-ued. "Our house is always open to you if you need to search for more information." Their hospitality warmed my heart. I didn't feel alone anymore.

As I packed, this Saturday morning seemed to drag. I was so eager to meet Estelle's relatives. Answers seemed so close, and I was too excited to concentrate much. I had to repack my bag and change into a light cotton skirt and T-shirt while I waited for Lita.

Once she arrived, we hurried outside and waved a hand, which stopped the southbound intercity bus. The vehicle was overcrowded, but we squeezed ourselves in. We had to push our way past trussed-up pigs, chickens, farmers with baskets full of freshly picked tomatoes, eggplant, and other vegetables I didn't recognize. Finally, we plopped down near the back, both of us sweating profusely

The long, hot ride on the open-aired bus was made even longer because it stopped several times to pick up passengers or let some off.

"I think the first thing we should do, Sue," Lita advised, "is to get off at the Catholic church and ask around about the Gonzales family. Here, people do not move often. And if it is the family home, they have probably been there for their whole lifetime and their grandparents' lifetimes."

"Won't people wonder why we're asking so many questions?" I asked. I feared strangers would be wary of us.

"Not really. My people care about each other, share gossip freely, and enjoy sharing information with each other. They'll admire your pretty fair skin and American demeanor. Your blonde hair attracts attention. It will give them something to talk about tomorrow."

I never thought of myself as a blonde, but maybe in this dark-haired nation, anything less than black could be labeled blonde.

"Lita, maybe we should first just be looking for Estelle. Let's not mention my dad, or all that other stuff. It's all so complicated. You could say I got a letter from Estelle and wanted to meet her."

"I think that would be a good idea. If this is the right family, we will probably know pretty soon." Lita was a girl of wisdom, I could tell.

My handkerchief was grimy with perspiration and dust from wiping my face, when I stuffed it back into my purse. I felt sweaty, dirty, and exhausted after only an hour or so on the bus. Finally, we stepped down into the bustling plaza area of Cabanatuan. My bag seemed several pounds heavier as I adjusted the strap over my shoulder and followed Lita into the crowd.

We stopped at several houses near the church and were finally directed to an old wooden structure, which was unpainted on the outside, but had carved work at the corners. It was completely fenced in with intricate, black wrought-iron work in a scrolled design and had matching window grilles—similar to the house the Davinses lived in.

Lita picked up a small stone and pounded on the metal gate, yelling, "*Tao Po! Tao Po!*" in a loud voice. We waited, and soon an old woman opened the large front door, peered out, and then descended the front steps of the porch to meet us at the gate.

"Is this the Andaya Gonzales home?" Lita asked politely, using the Ilocano language. The woman nodded yes and invited us in.

The gate screeched irritatingly as she slid the bolt across to open the gate to us. Meanwhile, she hushed a dog that was tied out of sight but was barking his best attack-dog imitation. The gate screeched again as she closed it firmly behind us.

The woman seemed to be about sixty-five or so and moved slowly as older people are prone to do. We entered the dark interior of the house, which seemed cool in comparison to the outside. A ceiling fan rotated lazily on its axis overhead, creating a breeze. Motioning for us to take seats in the living room, she unexpectedly left.

I looked at Lita with wondering eyes. "She's preparing something for us to drink or eat?"

"We never have visitors in our homes without food," she said.

When the older woman brought me a glass, I said, "Thank you," before I sipped the ice-cold Coca-Cola. It sure satisfied my thirst. Plain soda crackers came on a small plate too. We ate and drank in silence until the woman returned with her own drink.

Typical of any conversational event, the main reason for the visit was not immediately expressed. Lita, in true Filipino fashion, led in with, "This must be the Gonzales's family home. I seldom see such fancy iron grilles on homes here anymore."

"Yes, my in-laws lived here, and their parents before them. We were just fortunate it wasn't destroyed during the wartime."

"Would you be Mrs. Gonzales? We were told this was the home of the Gonzaleses."

"*Wen.*" She answered in the affirmative, using Ilocano.

"Is your husband Andaya?" Lita continued. I was in the dark linguistically but followed the expressions on their faces. "We were talking with David Wisco at Wisco Hardware in Muñoz. He said that Estelle, your niece who worked for him many years ago, moved down here to be with you. Are you the family who have a niece Estelle?"

"You mean Estrelita, I suppose. I never did like these strange shortened names that young people use. Yes, Estrelita lived with us for many years."

"This is my friend, Sue Gibson. She is an American, whose mother received a letter from Estrelita many years ago. She wanted to meet her."

"Estrelita got a good job at Phil Am Life in Makati and now lives down there," the woman informed us with pride. "She even sends us money each month to live on." Lita quickly translated this information for me.

Lita wanted to pursue the matter some more. "May I ask some questions about Estrelita? We want to know for sure this is the same person that wrote to Sue's mother."

"Wen," was the affirmative reply again. She didn't seem to be a woman of many words.

"Did Estrelita grow up in Gabaldon, or some remote barrio of Gabaldon?" Lita was using the more complex name to please this woman's tastes.

"Yes, she did. We never saw her until she was about sixteen years old and wanted to attend CLSU."

"Where did she go to school before that time?" Lita asked.

"I don't remember. There was no school where they lived."

"David Wisco said Estrelita had excellent English and was tutored by an American when she was young."

"Oh, you mean Joe," Mrs. Gonzales recalled. "I'd forgotten about him. Estrelita talked a lot about him. He must have been an exceptionally capable man. She often spoke about how much she loved and respected him. Yes, he taught her. She even passed the entrance exams at the university the first time!"

As Mrs. Gonzales seemed to be praising Joe, Lita translated for me in an undertone. My heart dropped to a new low. I felt my temper rising. *This was my dad, and he was already married. How could he do this? He was already happily married to my mother.*

"Would you be willing to give us Estrelita's address in Makati?" Lita asked.

"Where is Makati?" I asked Lita, during a break in the conversation.

"That's where you flew into Manila. It's actually the southern part of the Greater Manila area, and, in fact, is the financial center for the whole Philippines."

Mrs. Gonzales had left the room to find the address and paper to write down this information. Immediately, I planned to continue my quest south to Manila to find Estelle. This new information put me at even a lower ebb. I could now understand why my mother never showed me that letter and why she never admitted its existence. The painful fact must have been hard to accept. I put my hands over my eyes to weep inside for a mom who had to face this alone. I felt it was time for Lita and me to leave. We had the information we came for, but I felt sick at heart.

Then I heard the familiar squeaky gate. Someone must be coming home, maybe the man of the house this time, because the dog didn't bark.

SEVENTEEN

Estelle

Cabanatuan, July 1980

We all looked toward the door in anticipation. A pleasant female voice called, "Tiya, Tiya, I'm home!" A woman appeared in the doorway. I could only see a silhouette against the brightness outside. I got the impression of a slim, poised woman who was very much at home here.

The old lady, having just returned with the desired address, visibly brightened. She rushed to hug the woman at the door. "Estrelita, I'm glad you came home this weekend. There is a woman here who is looking for you." They hugged excitedly and warmly, much like mothers and daughters often do after a long separation.

Estelle blinked, trying to adjust her eyes to the darker room. She looked from Lita to me, not knowing which one of us was looking for her. "Have we met before?"

My adrenalin kicked in. This was the moment I'd come here for.

"Not really," I answered, speaking English. "But I've come to the Philippines to find you."

"Why is that?" she said, speaking English in a modulated and businesslike voice.

"I'm Sue Gibson. My maiden name was Sue de Cou. Does that remind you of someone?"

Her eyes widened in disbelief. She sat down in the nearest chair and let out a big breath. In fact, she seemed hardly able to speak. Much to my amazement, she gasped and started to cry.

"You must be Joe's daughter! I can't believe you would come all this way to see me. I've longed for news about you and your mother for so many years that I'd quit hoping." As she cried, she groped for a hanky.

"I only saw your letter to mom a couple of years ago after she died." I gulped. "Mom had put it away with all of Dad's letters, but she never mentioned it to me all the time I was growing up."

Estelle sipped the drink her aunt had brought her from the kitchen. "I wondered why I never heard anything from your mother or you. I had written to you with this address. It must have been when I was fifteen or sixteen, about the time I started college. Let me see, that was more than twenty years ago."

I looked at Estelle more carefully. She was not much older than I, a few years at the most. There could not have been an alliance of lonesomeness between my dad and her. She still would have been a child!

I no longer needed to sustain that erroneous suspicion about my dad!

"I, too, was confused by your letter, Estelle. My mother had been informed that dad was missing in action. He had never been found. After several years, she assumed he was dead. Then we got—or rather my mother got—this letter from you telling of your love for Dad and how much he meant to you. My mother must have thought . . ." My attempt to express the correct thought was more than I could utter.

"Do you suppose your mother thought your dad had shacked up with me?" she expressed succinctly and candidly. "I was just a kid, but of course, she couldn't have known that!"

I nodded yes. "I suppose those were her worst fears, and rather than pursue the matter, she just filed your letter away and decided not to say anything to me. Also, there was a strange collect phone call from Cabanatuan. It was cut off after only a few words. Mom wrote them down, but they didn't make any sense. This was with the letters too."

"My dad tried to call Wyoming once," Estelle said, "when he was in Cabanatuan. But because his English was limited, he didn't know if he was understood. I presume that was the call."

We had moved closer together as we talked. I was a sponge soaking up information. She was a dam let loose finally. Soon we were hugging, crying, and laughing together.

"Sue, I really wanted to meet you because I had your dad's love when you were unable to have it. He was a generous, giving man, even when seriously ill. I remember when I was about six years old, we had a little ceremony of our own. He formally adopted me as his daughter. So I became Estelle de Cou in my own mind, as well as his."

"Do you mind having a sister?" she asked. "For your information, I legally became Estelle de Cou a short time ago." Another reason for us to hug.

I definitely did not mind having a sister. I was delighted! Estelle exuded warmth and acceptance. She typified tropical beauty too. I was stunned by what a gracious woman she was.

Totally obsessed by our newfound relationship, we talked avidly for hours. I glanced at my watch. I hadn't noticed the fast-falling dusk. Lita had picked up a picture album and was thumbing through the previous history of this family.

"Please stay and eat with us, Sue, and you too, Lita." She had guessed what the glance at my watch meant. "My aunt is probably fixing a tasty dinner for us now. I know you can smell the mouth-watering aroma of sautéing garlic, ginger, onions, and pork. Just a minute. Let me ask her. I'll be right back. Don't go anywhere!"

I turned to Lita when Estelle left the room. "What do you think I should do? Go back with you, or . . .?" I asked.

"I think you should see if you can stay here with them and return to Manila with Estelle. She's the reason you came to this country, isn't she?"

"I feel a little embarrassed about this. I'll just have to hope that Estelle will invite me to stay." I grinned. "Will you stay to eat before going home yourself?"

"Yes, I'll stay with you. My parents will not be upset if I come in late," Lita reassured me.

Estelle came back into the living room. She had changed into a cool muumuu-style housedress.

"Tiya says you are both invited to eat with us. *Tiya* means auntie, Sue. We'll talk while we eat and decide what to do. I don't want to lose you so soon after we've met. But excuse me, I must help her a while." She left in the direction of the yummy smells.

My mind lifted toward the God who had definitely arranged this meeting at this time and in this place. Not a coincidence at all! I was all warm and tingly, glowing with appreciation. I was satisfied and so glad I had made the effort to travel to the

Philippines. I felt sure there was plenty more to learn about my dad from Estelle in the days to come.

I moved over to sit next to Lita, as we looked through the family photo albums on display on the coffee table. I saw pictures of a gangly teenager, who must have been Estelle in her early years in this house. She looked so shy.

After our great dinner of rice, plus the tasty vegetables I'd been anticipating, I sat back. My mind buzzed with ideas. What should I say? *Estelle, come back to Wyoming with me, so we can get to know each other.* In my estimation, life was so inadequate here. I couldn't express these feelings, though. Estelle seemed a happy, fulfilled woman.

"Estelle, what do we do now? I have another week before my flight back home?"

"Come to Manila with me," she said quickly. "I'll show you how I live now. I'll take time off work, and we'll visit all the places Joe talked about wanting to take you. Please! Please! You can be a tourist instead of a perplexed detective."

I grinned. That I'd truly been.

We were all worn out by the excitement. Shortly after we ate, Lita left for the long journey home. It was ten o'clock already. My eyes were heavy, as were Estelle's. After a refreshing cold shower, we crawled under the mosquito net and sleep came easily, even on that hard, unpadded mat on the shared bed.

EIGHTEEN

Joe de Cou

Manila, July 1980

On Sunday, Estelle and I sleepily boarded the 4:00 a.m. bus headed to Manila. This station was the starting point for the southbound Luxury Liner buses. The bus itself was newly washed inside and out, and the air conditioning was already humming.

"We want seats toward the back, which will be quieter and even cooler later on," Estelle advised. We settled into seats that even reclined.

"Tell me about those years that you had with my dad," I entreated, as our bus swung out into the nearly deserted road. Estelle seemed to ponder her answer.

We sailed through Gapan at a frightening speed, and I commented, "This bus has far less stopping and starting than the bus the other day. What a relief!"

Estelle finally spoke. "I was thinking how to describe to you the really primitive situation we lived in. All the years I was growing up we lived in just a simple hut, with bamboo slat floors—smaller than the size of this bus. Our beds were mats rolled out on the floor. There were no chairs or table. Water came from a stream or spring, depending on where we put our *bahay kubo*—native hut—that particular season."

"Did you move often then?" I asked in surprise.

"The crops, which were sweet potatoes, were too small to sell after a few seasons. So we would move onto another place that looked good, burn the hillside, cut the trees and bushes, erect another bahay kubo, dig up the soil, then replant and start again."

"That seems like a lot of work," I commented.

"It was. Hard work was the only life my dad knew. We barely subsisted from month to month and year to year. We hardly had enough clothes to cover us. Dad would go into the heavier forest for days at a time looking for animals or birds and bats to kill for food and for certain plants that we used for our medicines. I believe you call them herbs now, but I just knew Mom hung them in bunches in a corner of our hut. I had to drink that awful water the leaves were boiled in when I got sick to my stomach or had a fever. They seemed to work. I was their only child remaining alive after many pregnancies."

"I presume you had no bathroom?"

"No, when I was little and untrained, the slat floor was just sloshed down when accidents happened. Later we just used the outside. I never even experienced diapers. No one else was around anyway. I don't think I ever considered this odd until I came into the city where my aunt and uncle live, and they told me the necessity for using the bathroom for certain functions. I was, by then, in my teens. At that time, I truly began to realize how uncivilized I was. Tiya was very patient with me, teaching me modesty, appropriate eating behavior—"

"What do you mean by eating behavior?" I interrupted.

"Because we lived, ate, and slept on the same floor, when there was food cooked, we would fill a coconut husk bowl with the rice and soup, squat down, and devour our food with our fingers, then slurped up the soup. There were no utensils in my youth. I had never seen a table knife until I became acquainted with bread."

My mouth opened wide—dumbfounded. She stopped in the middle of her tale and looked at me.

"You don't believe me, do you?" Estelle questioned, putting her arm around my shoulders and drawing me close. "This is all true."

"How could you exist like that?"

"This basic home was all I knew. We had two or three pottery cooking pots, and an earthen jar for drinking water." She circled her palms as we would in describing the roundness of a volleyball.

I could then visualize a water pot as shown in old Bible story pictures I pored over as a little girl. This new sister of mine grew up similar to biblical times—with simplicity.

"What did your mom use to stir a pot when she cooked?"

"During the wetter months, when the crop was planted, dad would sit on the floor and whittle pieces of guava wood into useful spoons for this purpose. Guava is an easily available bush, but a really sturdy yet pliable wood and very hard to carve too. He'd also whittle his slingshot, or a bow and arrow. That seemed to be a man's job, so he never taught me the skill. But once Joe was strong enough, and my dad realized how ignorant he was in the basics of living, those two would sit on the floor, my dad training your dad, and whittling various items. It was there that I first learned what a stove looked like, or a bed, or even a light bulb. Joe whittled small ones for me."

"What did you use for light then?" I enquired. What a stark life!

"I wish I had brought out that cute little stoneware light . . . mmm . . . sort of like a flattened cream pitcher. Dad scraped and scraped for days on a soft type of stone to make this lamp for mom. She rendered out coconut oil, put it in the lamp, placed a piece of string in the oil, and left the end over the lip to burn for light. Most of the time we just went to bed when it got dark and got up when it was light, so the lamp was not needed."

"Truly, this is hard for me to visualize, Estelle, not having experienced it. I'm so used to a click of a light switch and, presto, I have light."

I continued my quest for information. "How did Dad react to living with you in that hut, with so little of anything?"

"Joe said something once . . . his philosophy: 'God does not place anyone where he had not planned him to be.'" Estelle was serious as she spoke. "It was several seasons, could have been a year or more. I was a child, and we had no calendars. It was a long time before Joe regained his strength and ability to function. All that time he would talk, not to us, but to a Being he seemed to know well. I was to find out this was the God who had planned this for him. No, Joe was neither surprised nor horrified at our living situation. He spoke every day to the God who placed him there." Both Estelle and I were very quiet at this point. A sermon by a deceased father.

God does not place anyone where he had not planned him to be. I repeated this profound statement to myself. A good one! In fact, one I had just heard the other day from a mother at her son's wake.

Estelle continued with her history. "I remember the first English word I learned—*good.* Joe would say that after eating Mom's rice and soup. He gained strength and could hold the coconut shell himself. I repeated the word 'good,' as he said it.

He glanced at me with a new understanding of the role he could play in my life. He smiled and we said it back and forth. Then I said *naimas*. He repeated what he heard—nah-EE-mas. We began to teach each other our own language. We used the hard-packed earth outside our hut as our blackboard. Soon I was learning numbers, colors, and sentences in English. He in turn learned these terms in Ilocano, the language we spoke.

"I do not believe any other child in the whole world had more wonderful first years of school. It was a school of two. We each taught the other. I would laugh at his attempts to speak my language, while it seemed I absorbed English fairly simply. Of course, I was five or six and he was thirty, so I suppose this made the difference. Your dad was such a fun man to be around; we played games and even sang songs." She paused in her long story.

"One place we went to about monthly was a stream where we went to wash our family's clothes once they got too stinky to tolerate. We'd made a small pool in the gravel to the side of that stream where we dumped that bundle of clothes to soak while we cooled off in the water after the long hike.

"'Look what I found, Essie,' Joe said once, extending his closed fist, palm side up. I ran over, expecting some creepy crawly, or bug. He opened his hand. There was nothing in his hand. I thought he was teasing me. 'Just look carefully.' I squealed as it seemed his palm moved then. 'It's translucent!' he explained. I looked again. 'It's . . . what . . . what did you call it?' I asked. 'I can't really see anything.' 'Translucent just describes this creature. It just means it is hard to see, or it's not transparent but clear enough to allow light to pass through.'"

I hung on her every word, eager to hear more about my father.

"Joe scratched his head for a moment," she said, "then his eyes lit up. 'Remember that large whiteish spider we found the other day?' 'Yeah,' I said, bobbing my head like any fourteen-year-old. I called it transparent. That wasn't its name. We could see right through it; that was a description of the spider. 'This is almost the same thing. Translucent means light can pass through, which almost makes it invisible. You might say, it almost can't be seen. I'll lay it on a dark rock and maybe this tiny little critter will be less invisible.'

"Yes, I could see something on the rock, but what?

"We started on the job of washing our clothes, using the bar of soap Mom and I had made, pounding each piece with our wooden paddle to get out the mud, or whatever. A fun job because we could be wet and cool at the same time. Then we laid them out on the large rocks to dry before going home.

"Joe said, 'There's thousands of these in our swimming hole. Let's take some with us when we return home. Essie, make one of those banana-leaf pockets to carry them in.'

"I cut a large leaf and laid it on a rock to wilt, so it would be more pliable, then fashioned our approach to a plastic bag, biodegradable even! We could more easily see the shape of these milky little whiteish creatures against the dark green leaf.

"I could tell Joe was trying to remember what this creature reminded him of.

"I was muttering these new words to add to my English vocabulary—transparent . . . translucent . . . invisible. We walked an hour home, with our bundle of clean dry clothes, smaller bar of soap, and also our envelope of . . . what?

"When we showed Mom our new acquisitions, she exclaimed, '*Lagdaw*, so delicious in soup.' She added them to our soup right away, and interesting enough, the critters turned pink. Joe said, 'I've had my first lagdaw, but I'm still trying to remember what I would call these in Wyoming.'

"Joe told me later. 'Just as I lay down after the exertion of the day, I remembered. I could almost imagine a light bulb popping on over my head, cartoon style. They were shrimp. Fresh water shrimp!'

"The next time we went on our washday trip, Mom prepared several large bamboo tubes so we could transport our lagdaw in water, so they would still be alive when we reached home."

"Tell me more," I said, almost giddy hearing about my father.

"That's what is so much fun about lagdaw salad. We just put soy sauce, calamansi juice—lemon juice—and salt on them. Then they are still jumping when we eat them. We call it jumping salad."

I suppose they called it salad because it wasn't cooked.

"Once, Joe fell off the cliff into the deep pool below. I thought he might have died. When I climbed down to the pool, I found he was fine. The pool was deep and cushioned his fall. So we considered this pool our secret swimming hole. Also our secret lagdaw source. We'd float in the water, looking up at the clouds and sky, enjoying the cool reprieve from the heat. The sun reflected off the wee shrimp, like gold flecks, as they swam. Every time we went there, Joe said the same thing. 'Essie, remember this is our own secret, golden swimming hole.' It was very poetic, but seemed a strange thing to say."

"When Joe suffered his final setback, one of the last things he said to me was 'remember our secret swimming hole,' then he placed one exquisite little Spanish gold medallion in my hand, about two centimeters round. I've kept that in my office drawer ever since." Estelle, wiping a tear running down her cheek, concluded this long story.

"He even taught my dad some interesting things," Estelle added, seeming to want to get past some of her more emotional memories.

"What would that have been?" I asked.

"Because of your dad, we stayed in the same *kaingin*—location—for many seasons. He suggested that my dad plant peanuts in the dryer months each year. Then dig up the peanuts, but instead of burning the plants, plow them back into the soil before we planted the *kamote* again—that's sweet potato." We giggled. "The next year's kamote crop was better and larger than previously. Soon other suggestions Joe made were added to our structured and unchanging existence. Joe said once that his college degree was in agriculture. Did you know that, Sue?"

"I only learned that when I got his bio data at the embassy. The papers said his college degree was in agronomy."

By now our eyes were heavy since we'd risen very early. My mind was filled with images of the father I never knew. We both laid our seats back and slept until the honking and heavy traffic as we entered Manila told us our journey was nearly over. I sighed as I opened my eyes. God was good. He brought me to the Philippines to find Estelle. She was such a lovely person, and we felt like sisters. And we talked about a man who'd been my dad, but had been hers, too, in a much more real way. I smiled in reminiscence.

NINETEEN

Goodbyes

Manila, July 1980

"I need to drop by my office first thing today to inform them of my absence this week," Estelle said on Monday, as we drank our coffee with *pandesal*, little hot rolls delivered every morning. "Won't take long, then we can catch the 11:00 a.m. hydrofoil boat out to tour Corregidor."

Estelle left her in the lobby, quickly hurrying off to take care of the request for leave. What I didn't know was that she then called her fiancé. "Chris, I've had something pretty exciting happen this weekend."

"Oh, what happened?" Chris replied.

"Remember, I told you Joe had a daughter, Sue? Well, she showed up in Cabanatuan at my aunt's place after all these years. Now she's with me. We're going to visit the popular tourist spots, places her dad wanted to show her. I'm taking this week off work."

"How very exciting for you; where are you going to take her today?"

"Probably Corregidor. But most importantly, Chris, you need to prepare your man to escort Sue Gibson and her assets when she flies back next Monday. The 8:00 a.m. flight on United, July 29, to San Francisco. I think that would be the best way to get her holding account safely to the US. But keep this quiet. Thanks, Chris."

The week that followed was filled with exuberance. We visited the other popular tourist spots in the area. The Manila Cathedral must have been one of those that dad mentioned in his letters. We toured Fort Santiago and the walled city where much fighting occurred during the war and where many Americans were incarcerated.

We talked constantly about Joe de Cou, my father, and Estelle's adoptive father. I learned more about the hardships of people living in this country. We took the hydrofoil boat out to Corregidor at the mouth of Manila Bay. We walked the old embattlements and explored the eerie tunnel where Americans held out against the Japanese for many weeks. Estelle, though she'd lived during that time, had not experienced the war.

I found it hard to think of leaving. My flight home was at eight o'clock the next morning. Estelle and I arranged to celebrate our meeting and soon parting with dinner at a fancy restaurant dressed up in the new clothes we were going to purchase together. This was to be a celebration of friendship and discovery.

So, we went shopping. This marketplace was unlike any crowded place I'd ever experienced. The first thing that struck me was the olfactory sensation, which made my eyes water. I supposed this came from the bales and bales of cloth stacked for sale. It was sort of like an enclosed warehouse with no ventilation.

"What's wrong?" Estelle asked, as I gasped for breath.

"Some smell seems to be getting to me."

"Oh, it's just the odor emanating from these fabric dyes. Some people are more susceptible than others. We'll move out to the edges of the market, where it will be easier to breathe. The ready-made clothes are displayed there anyway."

Like long-time separated sisters, we sorted through shop racks, looking for clothes for me to take home. I wanted items that would remind me of these days in the Philippines—days that had started with such disaster but were now ending so well. I examined the intricate and colorful embroidery down the front of long dresses. Which one should I choose? Clothes made here would hardly be warm enough in Wyoming, where the summer highs seldom reached the lowest temperatures I'd felt this past month.

Later, in a jewelry store, we sorted through earrings trying to find just the right pair to wear with my outfit. Then shoes were next. Alas, I could find no shoes to fit my size nine feet. Every store carried sizes only up to eight and a half. There were such attractive shoes in almost any color, style, and of good quality for such little money because of the exchange rate.

I did buy a pair of sandals, though, in size eight and a half, which fit me fine. They looked lovely with the peach-colored Filipina dress I purchased. Estelle bought a similar one in peacock blue. The heavenly blue color complemented Estelle's glossy black hair, tanned face, and fine features. Actually, we wore the same size, and I planned to send her something I'd purchased in the US.

After several hours of shopping, we dragged our bags to a taxi and drove back to Estelle's place.

Then we had another hour of enjoyment, like most women, as we went through our purchases. I'd bought far more than I would ever use. But I felt frivolous. Mainly, this was an investment in my time with Estelle, my beloved new sister.

In utter exhaustion we flopped on our beds that afternoon under a rapidly rotating ceiling fan to sleep for a couple of hours. I had found that waking up in a strong sweat made the rest unfruitful though. So I wrung out a soaked beach towel and draped it over my unclad body so that I could cool down to truly relax.

Estelle laughed at me and said, "My aunt would scold you and tell you that you would die of pneumonia!"

I had found out otherwise.

We woke to the sounds of a woman declaring her wares on the street: "*POO-toe, Poo-toe . . . Bee-BING-ka . . . Bee-BING-ka.*" I followed Estelle down the stairs to catch the vendor, and then we bought some sticky-looking items sold on a banana leaf. She called them *bibingka*, a most delicious combination of sticky rice, coconut milk, eggs, and brown sugar caramelized on the surface, which gave off an aroma like roasted coconut. The Filipino dinner hour is very late, and most people have what is called *merienda*—a snack—to tide over their stomachs until an 8:00 p.m. dining time.

We sat at the kitchen table, just the two of us, before her roommates returned from work and enjoyed bibingka and really cold refreshing soft drinks. Estelle had run down to the corner store to purchase them, as she had no refrigerator.

How in the world can she exist in this climate with no ice water, no place to store leftovers, no frozen vegetables or meat? But

I kept my thoughts to myself, admiring the spunk of my new sister who had come so far from an inaccessible jungle hut to her job in Manila and this livable place. She seemed so happy and satisfied.

Estelle talked of the man she wanted to marry. Chris was in his forties but still had not yet married, because he felt obligated to send his younger brothers and sisters through college.

My mind objected. *That's not fair to tie down the first professional in the family to so many years of financial obligation. Most families had six to nine children here, and that could be a lifetime proposition.* I knew few Americans with that kind of selfless dedication who would be willing to help their brothers and sisters through college. I admired Estelle's patience for waiting as well. She admired her man for his devotion to his family.

Meanwhile, she was saving money from her job so that they could maybe buy a home once they married. I gasped when she told me the price of a home and lot in this country, with little possibility of mortgages. The prices far outpaced the meager salaries most people received. I thought of the simple three-bedroom home I still owned, but now rented out. My mortgage was half paid for. *I'm so fortunate!*

This trip showed me a side of life that I could hardly imagine. I met people like Estelle, who felt she was fortunate to have water piped into her home; she appreciated the luxury of electricity. I, on the other hand, had become frustrated at the frequent brownouts, when we had to light our little smelly kerosene lamps. It was no more than a glass container filled with kerosene and then lit with a cloth wick. Quaint, yes. but it did not provide much light to read by, or study by. You had to move so close, it would be easy to burn your eyebrows. I laughed to myself when I recalled that someone had said the colloquial word for studying hard is "burning your eyebrows." I could now see why.

Later, Estelle and I pampered ourselves with manicures and hairdos at the simple home beauty parlor around the corner. It only cost me twenty-five cents in US money. I enjoy pretty hands, but I had never had a manicure back home. Here I had noticed most women, whether professional or otherwise, manicured their nails. Even their hair was neatly trimmed. Estelle opted to pull her hair back smoothly into a chignon at the nape of her neck, emphasized by a pretty black lace bow, a style which really complimented Estelle's classic Filipino beauty. She was such a lovely woman. When we returned home to dress for our big night out, we felt like two teenagers going on a date. But tonight there were no men involved.

Once Estelle put on her earrings, the picture was complete. I was amazed at those gorgeous earrings, long and dangly, intricate gold-filigree creations. "Those earrings are stunning. Did you buy them today?"

"No." Estelle hesitated for a few moments. "Actually, these earrings should be yours."

"Why?"

"Because your dad gave them to me. As I nursed him during those final months as he battled pneumonia and also, off and on malaria, he realized he would never be able to get enough strength to walk out to the road. He opened his wallet, which was now moldy, and took these earrings out of a piece of old newspaper.

"'These are for you, Estelle. I wanted to take them to my wife, but I don't believe I'll ever walk again. Here, they are yours to wear and remember our time together.'

"Even then I knew these were special," Estelle said. "They became even more special when I knew he was dying, and I realized these would be the only mementos of his time with us. I have Joe to thank for any education I got, and I'll never forget that gift."

I fingered the lovely earrings, thinking they looked like Spanish antiques. "They are truly exquisite, Estelle, but they're yours. My dad gave them to you. Keep them . . . please."

"Thank you!" She seemed to breathe a sigh of relief.

TWENTY

Our Final Dinner

Manila, Monday, July 28, 1980

We picked the Italian Village in Makati for our dinner that night. My heart felt heavy. I didn't want to leave Estelle. I'd learned so much about my dad and about her in recent days. But I determined not to be sad tonight. We were elegantly attired young women dressed in new clothes and shoes, with elegant coiffures and manicured hands. It was a night to celebrate!

We entered the room, looking for a vacant table. "*Dee-toe*," Estelle said, pulling out a chair for me.

"What does dee-toe mean, Estelle?"

"*Dito* means 'here,' in Tagalog," she replied. "Why?"

"That was one word that your dad used in that long-ago phone call from Cabanatuan. He said, 'Joe dee-toe.'"

My mother, not knowing what that meant, just wrote down what he said. That meant my father was here, in the Philippines, and my mother never knew. Information so vital, but sadly not understood.

After ordering pasta topped with a traditional sauce with mushrooms and capers, we munched on small individual loaves of French bread, still warm from the oven.

131

"There's something that has bothered me, Estelle. You said you studied at CLSU, but when I asked about you, they had no record of your studying there. I wonder why that is?"

I wasn't expressing doubt about her honesty, just puzzled. Estelle thought a minute, then emitted a little laugh.

"I know why. It's because of a superstition among us Ilocano people. When I was a child, I became deathly sick, and my parents changed my name to confuse the spirits. I've been called Estelle ever since. I was surprised when I looked up my birth certificate and saw that I wasn't Estelle at all, but Estrelita Maria Gonzales. So legally, I am Estrelita Maria, but I've always gone by Estelle, or Essie, for short."

"So that's why your Estelle name was never registered at CLSU. At times I'm really confused about your culture!" I laughed.

"Since I was an only child when my parents died, there was no one who really cared what I called myself. After I became a professional, I had my name changed legally to Estelle de Cou. Now I really confuse the spirits; I've been healthy most of my life. So it must work!" She giggled.

"Oh, Estelle, we truly are sisters. I wish I were taking you back with me to Wyoming." I gulped to push down the grief of separation. Our scrumptious dinner arrived, and I pushed away my sadness to enjoy our time together.

As we ate our pasta, we were probably thinking the same thoughts about the imminent separation. The food was delicious, and the restaurant was crowded with other diners, talking animatedly.

Over dessert, *Brazo ni Mercedes*—a sweet confection of sponge cake rolled up and topped with some sweet syrup—we discussed how to keep in touch with each other in the following months and years. We ordered cappuccinos to linger longer. The moment seemed solemn, but we didn't want our time together to end.

A man approached our table from behind me. When I turned around, it took a few minutes for me to recognize this suavely dressed man in this fancy Makati restaurant.

"Hello, Sue," he said. "Good to see you again."

My mouth fell open, literally. This was Sonny, my erstwhile tour guide and the man who had abandoned me at the hotel in Cabanatuan. I noticed Sonny was handsomely dressed in slacks and a Filipino dress shirt with polished shoes. Well shaven and groomed, Sonny seemed a different man. I was flattered to be recognized by someone. I knew few people in the Philippines, at least here in this city.

"I hardly recognized you, Sonny!" I gasped. "Let me intro-duce you to my . . . uh . . . friend, Estelle de Cou. Estelle, this is Sonny." I glanced up at him. "I guess I never knew your last name."

"Agraviador," he said.

"Sonny accompanied me to Cabanatuan when I first came to the Philippines looking for my dad," I explained to Estelle. "I felt so lost at the beginning."

"You certainly don't act lost now," Estelle said. "I'm glad to meet you, Sonny."

"You two must be celebrating. *Napakaganda kayong dalawa*! You two look absolutely stunning." Estelle translated for my information. "I wish I was your escort for the evening."

"I know you pretty well for your ability to flatter, Sonny." Not a very kind comment, I realized as soon as I said it. I put my hand over my mouth in embarrassment.

"I'm sorry," I blurted out. "That was uncalled for." Seemingly hurt by the rebuff, Sonny turned to leave. But then he turned around to speak with Estelle.

"Estelle, it was so good to meet you. Your earrings are gorgeous!"

"Thank you," she said with a smile. "They were a gift from a very special man. In fact, they were part of Yamashita's treasure."

Sonny stood speechless, a look of surprise on his face. Then slowly he turned and left the restaurant.

TWENTY-ONE

The Envelope

Manila Airport, July 29, 1980

"**S**ue, I brought a large envelope for you," Estelle said. "You could lighten your carry-on bag considerably if you put the tourist information you've collected in it and mail it home, rather than lug it with you through three airports."

Estelle pointed to the bulging bag with colorful brochures about Corregidor, the Bataan Death March, Baguio, Santa Thomas Church, and the pamphlet about Ifugao culture and lifestyle. Then she pointed to the thick packets of photos I had stuffed in my bag too.

"No, I'm not letting those photos out of my sight!" I protested. "I'll keep these in my purse. I think it's a great idea to mail this other heavy stuff to Powell though."

I opened my bag wider and found other mailable items. I pulled out a non-English Philippine newspaper, an article on local fruit, and a cassette of Philippine music. I handed these to Estelle, who seemed to have taken over the task of redistribution. Estelle placed another folded envelope among the stuff she was packing for me. She flattened the packet, then secured it closed. I wrote my home address on the outside. Estelle produced stamps, and I pulled my suitcase while we walked down to the mailbox.

I still had fifteen minutes before I needed to board. Estelle hugged another passenger she knew boarding with first-class passengers, then joined me.

"Thanks for thinking of that, Estelle. I know I'll be really tired of lugging around my bag by the time this long day is over. I'm tired even thinking about my thirty-hour flight coming up." The reality of my leaving hit me again.

When the boarding call came, Estelle and I clung to each other for a moment. No tears.

"I promise, I'll write you this week, Sue," Estelle promised. "And don't forget. You promised to write me too. I'll ask if I can call you from my office phone, but I'm not sure they will allow me to do that."

We fell silent. There was nothing more to say.

As I turned to take my place in line for the boarding ramp, I showed my passport and boarding pass to the agent. I was followed by an American family with three kids in tow, apparently returning home after several years abroad. The kids wore flip-flops, shorts, and old T-shirts.

I glanced back for a final good-bye wave to my new sister, but Estelle was being roughly grabbed by a man. It was Sonny! I turned to run back down the ramp, but the flight attendant stopped me.

"I'm sorry, ma'am, but you can't leave the line. You've already checked in!"

Shaking off the woman's firm hand, I yelled, "Please call security. My friend is being taken against her will. The woman in the bright blue blouse with the red purse!"

I pointed frantically toward Estelle as she was pulled out of sight. Against my will, I was firmly escorted onto the plane.

TWENTY-TWO

Be Prepared!

Manila Airport, July 29, 1980

Estelle recognized the look on Sonny's face—the same from last night. It was a lot more than admiration for a lovely pair of earrings. It was an I-want-those-earrings look. Somehow, she knew by instinct. His face reflected the lust of possession at any price.

Now she knew why he had grabbed her.

Estelle might have been a sheltered girl when she was young, but living in Manila, especially working in Makati, had taught her to be cautious, streetwise, and to plan for any assault.

Long ago in the jungle, Joe had taught her self-defense. Plus she had also taken self-defense training with the other women working in her office.

Meanwhile, Sonny hugged her tightly and dragged her toward the back-seat door of a car at the curb.

"Now that your sneaky friend has gone," he said, growling, "where did you get those earrings you wore last night?"

"A friend gave them to me, you creep. Let me go!" she yelled in Ilocano. Estelle struggled against him, but she couldn't free herself, despite her training. Still she fought against him as he pushed and shoved her toward the car waiting at the curb.

Sonny had her shoulders solidly in his grasp, but not her elbows and lower arms. Using all her strength, she smashed one elbow into his face, then used her other to hit him in the groin. Suddenly, he let go of her and doubled over in pain while Estelle escaped through the opposite side of the car as the driver pulled out into traffic.

The plane carrying her newfound sister Sue Gibson disappeared into the clouds above just as Estelle disappeared into the crowds surrounding the airport. Pumping her arms, she ran as fast as she could, weaving in and out of people saying hello or goodbye to friends in the busiest airport in the country. She prayed fervently for God's help to make her escape.

Hopping on a jeepney full of people, she didn't care which direction it took her, as long as it was away from the maniac chasing her.

Her desperation to escape was fueled by the fact that she *did* know where the treasure had been hidden so long ago and could be tortured to divulge that information. After jumping off the jeepney in the heart of the city, she kept running. Where could she go? Sonny probably knew where she lived. She couldn't hide there. But she needed to warn her roommates about Sonny. Because of her, they were in danger too!

TWENTY-THREE

Reassurance

United flight to San Francisco,
July 29, 1980

Boarding the plane, I was frantic and uncertain exactly what to do. I stepped into the alcove near the cockpit, letting the last two passengers enter to look for their own seats before me.

I stepped close to the flight attendant. "You've got to do something for my friend. She's been kidnapped! I saw a man dragging her out of the airport. I can't leave without knowing what has happened to her." My breath came in huge gasps.

The attendant calmly asked to see my ticket and checked my assigned seat. Then she led me down the aisle, reassuring me.

"We alerted airport security as soon as you told us. They will take care of the situation, I promise you. They will rescue your friend. But now you need to sit down. We've been cleared for takeoff momentarily."

What else could I do, except comply? If I didn't, they might arrest me for disrupting the flight. Stepping over two people who were already seated, I dropped into my seat next to the window. Putting my face in my hands, I moaned and cried as I prayed for Estelle's safety.

"Is there something I can help you with?" asked a pleasant voice beside me.

I glanced up at the planeload of people, realizing I was not alone in my misery. My eyes locked on the woman beside me.

"I've just lost my best friend," I said, sobbing. "She was abducted just as we entered the gangplank. What can I do?"

My seatmate gently placed a hand on my knee, squeezing ever so gently to calm me, and then she began to pray aloud.

"Lord, this woman has just seen her friend kidnapped," she prayed. "Please protect her friend from harm right now and bring assurance that even in these dire circumstances, you are still in charge. Amen."

I grabbed my neighbor's arm in gratitude. "Thank you so much. I know God will do that. He has protected me the last two weeks while I searched for what happened to my father during the war. I know He'll continue . . ." I burst into tears again. "My friend is Estelle, a sister I never knew I had. Well, not exactly a sister, but she's become a sister to me. It's so complicated that I can't explain it."

As the plane left the runway with a roar, I was pushed back in my seat by the swift ascent. Everyone sat quietly as our journey began . . . whether we were ready or not.

My seatmate leaned close and whispered, "We can talk later. I need to see how my kids are doing."

Settling into my seat, then arranging my purse beside me, I reclined, trying to relax in the realization that God had not abandoned Estelle even now. Half praying, half reminiscing, my thoughts raced through my head, remembering what God had done during the weeks I had visited the Philippines.

"God, you didn't abandon my mother after all. My dad couldn't come back to be the husband and father you sent to Asia. But Lord, you used my dad in the lives of another family who needed him. You taught them about yourself through this stranded airman. What a fantastic plan you set in motion through the life of another young girl who was my age!

"God, you didn't abandon me either. You provided the wisdom and practical help of the Davinses, the missionaries who knew people and places. They knew the language and culture. They were willing to help me in seeking information. You provided that, Lord. Thank you so much for caring for me, a foreigner alone in a strange country.

"Through the clue of a coed with exceptional English ability, you led me to Estelle and where she lived. What a miracle! In a country of a million people, you led me to the one my dad taught thirty-some years ago. Can you imagine! Thank you!"

With an involuntary intake of a deep breath, I finally drifted off into a peaceful sleep. Resting, trusting, and knowing that God would not abandon Estelle, I knew she would escape and sleep without panic or fear. As I drifted into twilight sleep, I remembered a verse from Isaiah 41:12–13:

> *Though you search for your enemies,*
> *you will not find them.*
> *Those who wage war against you*
> *will be as nothing at all.*
> *For I am the Lord, your God*
> *who takes hold of your right hand,*
> *and says to you,*
> *"Do not fear; I will help you."*

God's Word reassured me that Estelle's welfare was in His hands and that He loved her far more than I ever could. She was His child, and He would take care of her.

TWENTY-FOUR

A Letter and Aunt Frances

Powell, Wyoming, November 1980

F our months later, I received an airmail letter from the Philippines. I rapidly glanced at the return address: The Davinses in Muñoz.

Pulling open the three flaps, I read:

Dear Sue,

We've not heard from you since your visit. Lita told us you'd found the woman you came to the Philippines to find. How wonderful!

But I'm writing because Lita came by yesterday asking us if we'd heard any word from you. The Gonzales couple in Cabanatuan came up here to Muñoz to ask David Wisco if he'd had any contact with their niece Estrelita. They haven't heard from her since she left with you several months ago. They wondered if maybe Estrelita went with you to the US. Did she?

They were worried because Estrelita visited them regularly to see how they were doing prior to your visit.

*Money in the same amount still comes each month from
her, but from a different bank and name: EDC Verzosa.
They don't know anyone by that name.*

*Please answer immediately so we can alleviate the worry
of this Gonzales couple.*

In Christ,
Lester and Pearl Davins

*P.S. We enjoyed your time with us. Sorry to lay a worry
on your shoulders.*

I knew that I had thanked the Davinses for their great help
in a letter. Now where and when did I mail it? Must have been
in the bunch of letters I left with Estelle to mail from her office
when she went back to work. Which probably meant she'd never
gone back to work. No wonder my friends didn't know I had
arrived in Powell. They never received my letter.

ⓢ   ⓢ   ⓢ

I lifted the phone as it rang one morning. "Sue, this is your
Aunt Frances in Billings. I'm driving down to get all the exciting
news about your trip to the Philippines. I'll come in about noon
tomorrow. Looking forward to seeing you."

"Aunt Francis, good to hear from you, but I'm just not up to
having company right now."

"Nonsense, honey, I need to see you. I'll be there tomorrow. Bye!"

The phone went dead.

Hanging up, I sat down, feeling lethargic and worried. I'd
felt little inspiration to do anything since I returned home. My
mind was always on Estelle.

At 11:30 a.m. the next morning, a beige Toyota pulled into my driveway. Aunt Francis. I sighed deeply. My house was a mess. My life was a mess. I didn't want to talk about my trip. Talking about it only made me feel more helpless. I knew I had laid the whole situation in God's capable hands, but still I worried.

Opening the door wide, I welcomed my aunt with a great big hug, remembering how my own mother had hugged me—a genuine hug filled with warmth and love. I started to cry and searched my pockets for a tissue.

"I'm so glad you came!" I said, sobbing. Aunt Frances put her arm around me and stepped inside out of the cold. She closed the door and then removed her coat, gloves, and sweater, and threw them on the sofa.

"What's wrong, honey?" Aunt Frances asked. "Why are you crying? I thought you had a good time on your trip. Did you start a relationship with a man, and it didn't work out?"

"Not in the way you might think," I said, sniffling. "You knew I went there to see what happened to my dad so long ago. You knew, didn't you, that Dad had been declared missing in action about the time I was born? No news. Nothing. Then some years later, my mom got a strange phone call and a letter, supposedly about my dad. I found these letters that Dad had sent to Mom." I gulped, then hesitated.

"Well, did you find him, Sue?" my aunt insisted.

"I found the girl of the family that found Dad in the jungle. They nursed him back to health. This happened in such a remote area, and he was so weak, that he couldn't walk out to inform us that he was still alive. Then Dad died."

"How did you manage to find that girl?"

I brightened a little as I explained the miracle of how Dad teaching Estelle the English language had helped me locate her.

"You see, my dad was Estelle's sole teacher. In the jungle, they lived in the most primitive of conditions. He was a teacher with no classroom, no pencil and paper, no blackboard, and no desks. He had absolutely nothing we have come to expect in grade school.

"But Dad had a good mind, and Estelle's youth and willingness to learn made for an ideal education setting." I paused to take a breath. "He even taught the family about God and His protection during his jungle experience. Dad was able to benefit Estelle's father with his knowledge of agriculture. Because of his knowledge, the family's planting and harvesting of sweet potatoes, highland rice, and peanuts improved.

"Later, Estelle's English usage was so exceptional that she stood out in college, and even in the college town she lived in."

Aunt Frances interrupted. "Why didn't you bring this Pebbles Flintstone back with you? She could have helped you clean up this house and the yard you're neglecting."

I defended my sister. "Estelle was not a *Flintstone* in any way when I met her. She's now an accomplished executive in a banking firm." I paused in my tale, not sure I wanted to continue, but I did.

"At least I still think she's a banker. The reason I cried when you got here is that Estelle disappeared when I left the Philippines. I saw her being abducted right at the airport. But there was nothing I could do about it. My plane flew out, and I was trapped on a thirty-hour flight. I've heard nothing from Estelle. She promised to write. But there's not been one word from her. She was like a sister to me. We talked nonstop for a week. We visited the places Dad had said he wanted to take Mom and me once he got out of the service." Slumping down into my comfy armchair, I quit talking.

Aunt Frances put a loving arm around me. "Is there any way I can help?"

"I don't know how." I sat in thought.

"Let's have lunch and see what we can do around here first. You need help," my aunt suggested.

Tuna-fish sandwiches made a satisfying lunch. I remembered jumping salad, which would never jump here. I didn't think Aunt Frances would appreciate hearing about eating raw shrimp anyway.

After lunch, my aunt immediately pulled out the vacuum cleaner to tidy up the neglected living room and hall, while I cleaned up the kitchen.

Aunt Frances evidently didn't think I had arranged my living room correctly, so when I joined her, I hardly recognized the room. She had turned the sofa at a different angle, moved a casual chair across from it, and placed the lamp on a different side table.

I gasped when I saw the change in the room. "This looks great, Aunt Frances. Looks like someone else's living room. Thanks so much."

She shrugged and smiled, then went back to vacuuming.

She dusted all the books in the bookcase, before placing the packet of Philippine tourist stuff out of sight in the hall closet. *I don't need any more reminders of that trip.*

"Hasn't your friend written or phoned you since you got back?"

I shook my head no. "She promised to write that next week, but I never received a letter. I never saw any phones except in the airport. Even the missionaries in central Luzon didn't have a phone. Estelle said she'd call from her office. That didn't happen either. I've been so worried, but I didn't know what else to do. I don't have the money for another airplane ticket."

God had sent help when Aunt Frances drove down to my place. Sometimes it is just the presence of your loved one who helps the most. They love, and care, and hug, and even clean your house, or fridge. I felt so much better since Aunt Fran showed up.

I should have known to call her when I first got home.

TWENTY-FIVE

Pastor's Advice

Powell, November 1980

P astor Roth approached me the next Sunday morning. "I sure appreciate your sharing with our class about your trip to the Philippines. I can see God truly led you in amazing ways. We'll be praying for Estelle." His comment was sincere and encouraging.

"But Pastor, I can't understand why that happened to her. I'd just found Estelle, gotten to know her, love her, and then lost her." I bowed my head in grief.

"Don't you think God is involved in our endings as well as in the process? Even when we don't understand?"

"Of course," I answered. "But why would He pop that exciting bubble of discovery? I feel so shattered now."

"I don't know why things turned out the way they did. Hopefully, we'll know in the future. That's what faith in God is all about." Then he lowered his voice and put his hand on my shoulder. "Sue, you're still the same woman I used to know, the one who could tackle a bull moose in her backyard." He smiled. "Keep trusting God through this. And we'll all be praying for a good outcome. Okay?"

I nodded my head, but at that moment, my faith was smaller than a mustard seed.

§   §   §

Another airmail letter from the Philippines arrived a few days later. I ripped it open. Even though I didn't recognize the name on the envelope, I hoped it carried news of Estelle. I was no longer confused after reading it.

> EDCV and Associates, Lagdaw Enterprises
> PO Box 1280
> Pasay City, Manila, Philippines
>
> Dear Mrs. Sue Gibson,
>
> We are pleased to announce our new business venture opening this month.
>
> Finding that Lagdaw could become a lucrative concern in expensive restaurants in Manila and elsewhere, even Hong Kong, we have now joined forces in our family to promote our product.
>
> Do not contact us. We are still trying covert operations, primarily, until the source is depleted, and we no longer face competition in that locale.
>
> We announce our wedding as of May 22 this year. Wish you could have been here.
>
> We send our best wishes to you and yours. Looking forward to seeing you. Look up Psalm 94:19.
>
> EDCV

It *must* be from Estelle, I thought after reading it a second time. EDC must stand for Estelle de Cou. Did she marry someone . . . someone with the last name beginning with V? I picked up my Bible from the coffee table to read Psalm 94:19. Flipping through the thin paper, I found the right page and ran my finger down to the reference. It read: *When anxiety was great within me, your consolation brought me joy.*

My heart leapt in my chest. The letter *had* to be from Estelle!

TWENTY-SIX

Prospector Account

On what are you basing this confidence of yours?
On whom are you depending? . . .
We are depending on the LORD our God.

—Isaiah 36:4–5, 7

Powell, December 1980

The Lord had given me another nugget of encouragement this morning. Realizing I was not in any emotional state to return to teaching this semester, I heaved a sigh of relief after phoning the school to tell them of my decision.

I had just hung up the phone when it rang again. "Hello?"

"Is this Mrs. Sue Gibson?"

"Yes."

"This is Steven Honor at First National Bank. We need you to sign some papers regarding your holding account. Could you come down this morning?

"Yes, I can come, but what's that? What's a holding account?"

"I'll explain when you come in. Will 10:00 a.m. today work for you?"

"I suppose—"

"Good. I'll see you then." He hung up before I could protest or question him further."

Later that morning, I met Steven Honor at the door of the bank. He was a tall man dressed in a dark, pinstriped suit, white shirt, and rather uninteresting tie. Then he escorted me to a small private room with a comfortable chair in front of a desk.

Placing an unopened black folder in front of him, Steven said, "These accounts normally start with what we call prospector accounts. Since you live in Wyoming, you understand who prospectors are. Right?" He continued without giving me time to answer. "These are ambitious young men, usually, who have a few gold nuggets in a bag. They've kept them in their pockets, or under their mattresses, always afraid they will lose them." He stopped to take a quick breath, and I nodded.

Clearing his throat, Mr. Honor continued. "Our bank has set up these simple accounts, primarily in prospector states, as we call them—Montana, Wyoming, Idaho, for example. Prospectors can bring in each little find as they discover them and deposit them in the bank."

"What's this got to do with me?" I asked.

He held up his hand and gave me a tight smile. "Please let me finish. Prospectors are not normally settled in one place. They hop from one site to another, looking for hot new mines, sometimes hitting it rich, often not. That's where we come in. Unfortunately, some young men try to double the worth of their sack of gold nuggets and get lured into one gambling venture or another."

The man seemed to be gathering steam. What did any of this have to do with my meager bank account at First National Bank of Powell, Wyoming? I yawned. Evidently, he finally realized he'd lost my attention.

"Mrs. Gibson, hang in there with me, okay?"

"But I really—"

"You need to understand this information," he interrupted. "I'll try to be more concise."

"Yes, please do."

"All right. First National soon set up growing prospector accounts in banks across this area to protect our clients' small assets. These accounts could not be accessed."

I shook my head. "Wait a minute. That doesn't make any sense. What's the use of a bank account if you can't access it?"

Mr. Honor held up his hand again like a stop sign. I was getting really frustrated at this point.

"Well, they're not inaccessible forever, just for a certain period of time. Because prospectors often disappeared, were lost, or died, these accounts—"

"Oh come on, Mr. Honor," I protested, standing abruptly. "I'm neither a real, nor a dead, prospector. Why did you call me down here?"

The now frazzled-looking man opened his black folder and then read a few lines. "Your name is on a prospector account, which is now called a holding account. Let me see . . . holding account in the name of Susan de Cou-Gibson . . . now fifteen years . . . maturing . . . six figures." He stopped.

My eyes widened. Six figures. In my ignorance, my mind registered $1,000.00. That would really help me financially right now.

"This type of account is normally set up by wealthy people to keep their spendthrift offspring from spending all their inheritance before they can get their hands on it. The accounts are usually locked down for fifteen to twenty years."

I blinked. Mr. Honor continued. "Your account was unique in one way. It was held by a young woman, who brought in some gold earrings and medallions, as the initial 'bag of gold nuggets,' you might say. We don't usually deal in the final product, but gold is gold. This deposit came to us from a foreign account. We'll need your number for this holding account."

"Did it originate with a Miss Estelle Gonzales?" I asked.

"Yes, yes," Mr. Honor smoothed his file. "Yes, that's the name here. Very good, Mrs. Gibson. Now we're getting somewhere. I was wondering how to explain your father's . . . ah . . . Mr. Joseph de Cou's . . . initial deposit by Miss Estelle Gonzales at First National Bank in Manila, the Philippines, which was transferred from the city of Cabanatuan there."

My mind wandered. *Those earrings must have been worth at least several hundred dollars, even back then!*

"Didn't the account earn any interest in that time?" I asked.

"Well, yes, yes, but very little. The risk is so high . . . risk of loss of ownership. As I said, prospectors seemed to disappear often."

All I heard at this point was a blur. His nonstop explanations were quite maddening. Butting in on his monologue, I asked, "When can I meet with a financial advisor?"

He looked at his schedule. "We can arrange that just after the new year, January 2, Friday. Is 10:00 a.m. all right for you?"

Then I recalled a fact Mr. Holder mentioned. I would need an account number. I didn't know I had an account, let alone have a number for one. Now what?

TWENTY-SEVEN

Financial Advisor

Powell, January 1981

I entered the room at the bank, looking around for the man I was to meet. A good-looking man in his thirties, wearing a dark-gray wool suit worn over a paler gray dress shirt, walked in and threw his overcoat on a spare chair.

"Mrs. Gibson, I am J.R. Verzosa, your financial advisor. I'm here to help walk you through a lot of decisions." His handshake was firm as he scrutinized me carefully with his eyes. "We will work together over these matters until they are clear to you—how these investments originated, the interest accrued, how best to handle this unusual account."

"I'd appreciate any help you can give me. Talking with Steven Honor, the bank manager here, I seem to have acquired a bank account. I didn't even know it existed, and by strange means, and I hope, honest means, and over many years. I hope you can help me understand this."

"That's what these sessions are all about. I hope we can meet each week for about an hour, and I'll try to explain the ins and outs of holding accounts and how yours will affect you."

I breathed a sigh of relief.

"Let me explain," he said. You didn't know it, but I was on that plane with you the day you flew from Manila to Wyoming. I was already seated in first class and anticipating my first trip to the US. I didn't realize it at the time, with all the screaming and crying, that *you* were my client. The entire first-class section was on red alert, anxious about what was going to happen on that flight."

"Oh, wow. I'm sorry to have introduced you to America in such an alarming manner! I'm truly sorry." Sue was embarrassed.

"I was personally escorting your holdings from Manila to Powell. They were more significant than a simple American Express transaction from bank to bank. Yours were . . . tangible . . . so discovery of their existence by the wrong people could cause a major military and media frenzy. I was instructed to remain anonymous."

I nodded my head. I had seen the violent effect, but apparently J.R. had not.

"I've typed up an orderly process we will follow," J.R. continued. "We need to become acquainted too. Look over these papers this week. Can you meet me here again next week at 10:00 a.m.?" J.R. passed a business card to her. "This is my temporary address and phone number in case you have any questions as you read through these ten pages prior to that time."

§   §   §

The following week, wanting to know more about J.R., I asked him, "What got you interested in finance and banking?"

He smiled. "I suppose we can take a few minutes to get to know each other. Let me see . . . when I was young, my dad was a tenant farmer just north of Manila. We could hardly make ends meet with five growing kids, living on his meager income. Once I started high school at thirteen the real trouble began. I found out I enjoyed studying, especially math and problem-solving. My father said he needed all of our help during the harvest. That job was hard, hot, and itchy.

"I rebelled. I wanted to stay in school. We had frequent fights and even came to blows. I would get out of the house before my dad was up at 5:00 a.m., then go to school with nothing to eat. My older brother, Cristopherson, who had just entered the employ of a bank, took me in, and paid my dad to hire a harvester. I decided then banking was for me too."

"I've heard of similar situations in Manila," I said, "and even here in Wyoming during roundup time when cattle need to be gathered from distant pastures, then counted, new calves branded, sorting for butchering, etc. All strong-bodied help is needed then, and ranchers take their teenagers out of school to help."

"Interesting! Two cultures, but similar conflicts!" he commented.

"Because I had no brothers, or even sisters, this didn't happen in my family," I said.

"We seem to be polar opposites as far as family size goes." J.R. then looked down and opened his briefcase.

"Let's look at what you're here for." J.R. laid out some papers on the table across from her. "Here are the documents regarding your original prospector account. Did Steven Honor tell you about that?"

"Well, yes, in detail . . . on and on and . . ." She looked to see if Mr. Honor might be listening at the door. "It seemed strange to have an account in the bank that gave little or no interest. Hardly a savings account!"

J.R. smiled. He had a great smile.

"You might call this a safety account. This account . . . mmm . . . your prospector account, originated here in Powell, Wyoming."

My eyes opened wide. "How did that happen?"

"Joe de Cou, your father, when he was a teenager, did some gold panning, as did many other teenagers then. He opened an account, really quite minimal value-wise, but it was a smart thing to do. Then he wasn't tempted to spend it on dates, adventures, or foolishly.

"This bank," he continued, "kept his few gold nuggets safely until maturation five years later. The war took your father away, but that nest egg stayed safe in this bank.

"American Express informed us from a bank in Cabanatuan in about 1954 or '55 that Joe de Cou was adding to this account in the Philippines. Arrangements were made to expand the arena of his prospector account, which was now accruing a much better interest per annum."

I must have looked a little glassy-eyed. "Are you following my line of thought, Sue?'

"I'm just not very good with numbers and banking stuff." I looked across the table at J.R. "You mean, our family was becoming rich and we didn't know it?

"Well, yes, in a way," J.R. said.

"I read these pages you typed up for me. I'm more confused now than I've ever been. Can you explain mutual funds, dividends, equities, cash, and equivalents?"

"The best thing you can do now is just trust that the bank, and me, as their employee and your financial advisor, is to keep your funds in such a manner that you can live comfortably.

Your money will be invested profitably. I'm here to protect your interests.

"Actually," he added, "I'm glad to do this for you in exchange for something you can do for me."

"What could that be?" I asked.

He looked chagrined. "You can teach me to drive. I've never had a car or felt the need for one. Manila has a lot of taxis and public transportation. While here, I'm pretty well stuck without a car."

I laughed. "That will be a lot easier for me to do than figure out this banking and money stuff."

"Great! Let's plan a time to go down to the car shop, or whatever you call it here, and look around for one I can buy."

I grinned. "Better yet, let me pick up some pamphlets from the Chevy dealer, showing a selection of sedans that you might like." Thinking a moment, I added, "Maybe I'll buy myself a new car, too, now that I'm independently wealthy. I'll have to ask the advice of my financial advisor, of course." She felt the warmth crawl up her cheeks. "We'll get two cars for the price of one. Almost like buying shoes."

Unexpectedly, he draped his arm around my shoulders, seeming to enjoy the joke as much as I did. And I didn't mind that we were flirting either, although I was surprised at my attraction to him.

"This protecting your interests is becoming more interesting all the time. Well, when can we go car shopping?" he asked.

We set the time and day for later the next week.

TWENTY-EIGHT

Bummer Lambs

Powell, Spring 1981

I woke to the demands of my alarm set for 4:00 a.m. Putting on warm pants, boots, sweater, and a heavy coat, I ate a quick oatmeal breakfast and was out the door in a few minutes. Clara Slack needed my help this morning with the bummer lambs.

Later, I strode into the bank rubbing my hands together vigorously. "I don't think I'll ever get my hands warm again!" I said to J.R. as I sat down in the chair.

"Why, don't you have enough heat in your house?" he asked.

"It's really cold in the barn. I've been helping my friend, Clara Slack, feed eight bummer lambs. Preparing bottles every four hours is a difficult job for a sixty-five-year-old woman."

"What are bummer lambs?" J.R. looked puzzled.

I needed to think a moment to explain these lovable, but needy, furry creatures. "They're newborn lambs that have been rejected by their mothers. They won't get near them, let alone let them nurse."

"What happened to their natural motherly instincts?" he asked.

"Maybe the mother had a difficult birth, or a second lamb came along and she neglected the first one. Actually, many reasons. These baby lambs will die within a short time if not brought to Clara for nurture and feeding. Ranchers bring them to her."

J.R. seemed interested, so I continued. "Clara built a frame to hold milk-bottle-sized feeders with large nipples. We introduce the infants to this mother feeder, and once they get the hang of it, after a lot of cuddling, consoling, and coaxing, plus hunger, and very loud baaa-ing, they start sucking. They are real suckers!"

They both laughed.

"I was amused to find out Clara names each bummer lamb once it survives the first few days. I was feeding Pinocchio, Pamela, and Stinky this morning."

J.R. threw back his head and laughed even harder. "I've got to see this!"

"I'll take you with me sometime and you can help. I'll never forget the first time I helped Clara with feeding the lambs."

J.R. looked skeptical. "I'm trained as a banker, Sue. I really don't have any desire to feed baby lambs."

I scooted closer to him and looked into his dark eyes. "Let me tell you something amazing about them. Once you've cuddled them, nursed them, and talked to them, they never forget you. I was out at Clara's ranch one time last fall, when something large bumped into me from behind. I turned to see Blacky, a full-grown ram, who was greeting me. He'd heard my voice and recognized me from when he was a bummer lamb. That was quite a reunion.

I took a chance and talked about my faith. "I recall Jesus Christ himself, saying much the same thing. Let me see if I can remember . . . 'the sheep follow him because they know his voice.' John 10, I think. Can you imagine, J.R.? We can actually recognize God himself because He cared for us when we needed Him the most."

"You've convinced me. I'll come out and take a look at your surrogate family, though they are furry little beasts." I laughed at his terminology.

I tilted my head and looked at J.R., a smile on my lips. "You can be a pretty likable person once you get out of your banker persona." I felt a flush spread up my neck, to my face, and clear up to the roots of my hair. I turned away, hoping to hide it.

"See this sweater I'm wearing?" I said, changing the subject. J.R. raised his eyebrows. "This is wool from those bummer lambs. I helped shear them, spun the wool into yarn, and then knit my own sweater. Feel it. It's amazingly soft, and there's nothing warmer in these Wyoming winters." I slid my arm across the desk so he could check.

J.R. touched my sweater and then pulled his hand away as if it had burned him. He cleared his throat and leaned away. "Tomorrow's the day we go car shopping and spending money we can afford."

His reaction surprised her a little, but I smiled inside. The color in his cheeks overrode his terse reply.

§   §   §

"This is the first time I've shopped for a car," I said. "Doing this together will be more exciting."

I drove across town to the Chevy dealership while J.R. sat in the passenger seat, reading the colored pamphlets about the different cars they could buy.

"I'd prefer something simple like this one." I glanced over a moment as he pointed to a beige sedan. "I think I've had enough of outrageously colored jeepneys. What are you thinking about buying, Sue?"

"I would love a red car if they have one. One that looks like the one you like." I pulled into the dealership. The salesman came out to greet us, almost before we got out of the car.

"What can I show you today? I'm Mark, and you are Mr. and Mrs. . . .?"

J.R. broke in, looking a little embarrassed. "I'm J.R. Versoza and this is Sue Gibson, a business associate. We're here to look at new cars." He produced the pamphlets with the cars we were interested in.

"Follow me, and I'll show you what we have."

We followed Mark out to the lot filled with cars of all makes and models and all new. J.R.'s eyes grew wide. "I don't think they import this many cars to the Philippines in a year's time. How am I going to choose just one?"

A couple of hours later, even after opening doors, enjoying the new leather smell, and sitting in perfect seats, J.R. was still undecided. I found my red car first in just the right size. J.R. was still in shock at the multiple choices, prices, and options.

"Do I have to make a decision today?" he asked. "I'm tired of so much to look at, and how wealthy I feel buying a car just for myself. I must be in culture shock."

"How about this," Mark suggested. "I'll bring the three or four cars you seemed most interested in around to the front. Come back later, look them over, think about it, and then buy the car you like the most."

"That would probably be a good idea. I have to learn how to drive and get my license first anyway."

Turning to me, Mark said, "And you, Ma'am, will you be buying that red Chevy you liked?"

"Yes, that's the one I want." I grinned at the thought of buying the first new car I'd ever owned.

"Then will you be using your present car as a trade-in?"

I had anticipated his question. "No, my pastor's wife could really use a car of her own. I'll just give it to her."

It took a while longer to finish the paperwork necessary. "We'll deliver your car to you tomorrow, Mrs. Gibson." Mark said.

As we walked slowly to my old car, I said, "We need to go by the DMV—Department of Motor Vehicles—to pick up a manual that you will need to study. Then you'll be tested on the information. Also, once you've learned how to drive, you'll need to take a driver's test, too, before you can get your driver's license."

Before I started my car, J.R. said, "I believe you are friends with a good friend of mine in Manila."

"I don't really know too many people there. I was only in the Philippines for two weeks or so."

"I got a short letter from her this week," he said. "She told me she'd sent you one too."

Then it dawned on me. "You mean Estelle de Cou!" I grabbed J.R.'s forearm. "She's a friend of yours?"

I felt the blood drain from my face as I looked into his eyes, "Oh, no, you're not the man . . . the man Estelle was planning to marry for many years. I don't believe it. She was so excited by the plans you'd made, the house you'd buy." Then I had to turn away because of my disappointment.

Using his forefinger, J.R. turned my face toward him. "No, no, no. You've got it all wrong, Sue. Estelle married my older brother Christopherson. After the wedding, I didn't hear from them for several months, then this letter came about a new job venture. I suppose that was what had taken up their time since last fall."

When relief washed over me, I knew our attraction was real.

On the way to the bank, we didn't say much. J.R. broke the silence. "Now let me tell you something you'll be happy to hear. Prepare yourself."

"What? I can't imagine being happier than I already am."

"Estelle is flying in next week. My brother Chris is coming with her."

"Really! That's wonderful." I think I may have squealed in my excitement.

J.R. chuckled.

I suddenly had a revelation. *I can ask her about the bank account number!*

I was savvy enough now to know that six figures didn't mean five little zeroes following a one. My inheritance was more than a $1,000.00. There were a lot more zeroes than that.

My holding account was worth a fortune!

TWENTY-NINE

Meeting Again

Powell, November 1981

Before Estelle and Chris's arrival, I purchased the warmest coat and pants I could find for Estelle. I didn't know Chris's size, but figured he must be quite a bit smaller than the typical Wyoming man. I got out the warm clothes I still had of Bob's. They would probably be too large, but at least they would keep him warm for the time being.

Finally, the day came for their arrival. "Have you found a warm coat for Estelle?" J.R. asked.

"Yes, I found the cutest blue parka lined in fur for her. She'll look lovely in it."

J.R. and I were waiting for them at the airport. I couldn't wait to see her. Then they walked into the airport, and Estelle and I ran to each other, hugging and kissing each other. Tears stung my eyes.

"I can't believe you're here," I said.

"I can't either." She pulled a tissue from her purse and offered me one as tears streamed from our eyes.

Soon, it was time to get on the road. Estelle slipped into her new parka before we exited the main doors. The wind blew in brutal gusts across the plateau. We scurried to my car with her carry-on luggage, while the men waited for the baggage to arrive on the carousel. A friend of mine from church waited in his pickup large enough to carry all their luggage and to give J.R. and Chris a ride home.

"Estelle, I'm so thrilled you're here!" I gave her another big hug after I started the car to warm it up. "I can't tell you how much I'm glad you're safe and that you finally married your Chris."

"His was the first place I ran to when Sonny grabbed me," Estelle explained as we pulled out of the Powell airport. "I frankly didn't know where else to go. I was so scared he would find me if I went back to my apartment. Once the news and pictures were broadcast about my abduction, the employees at the Manila Hotel identified you as the last person seen with SOA, as they called him, at that hotel. So they implied that you must be an accomplice. I didn't dare contact you in any way. I'm so sorry that I put you through that awful suspense. I know it must have been horrible."

"No more horrible than your struggle with Sonny, I'm sure," I said. "How did you get away?"

"With wits, speed, and training." Estelle giggled. "Joe had trained me well in self-defense. By the time your plane hit the clouds overhead, I'd disappeared into the crowds outside the airport. Gone . . . disappeared . . . vanished!" She clapped her hands together in a swishing motion and laughed in triumph.

"Weren't you scared?" I said, glancing at her.

"You bet I was scared, but it sure drove the sadness of your leaving out of me in a hurry."

As she filled me in on her escape, I drove across the crest of the bluff, then a few miles down into Powell.

"Not much green around here," Estelle said. "Not even trees or gardens. This seems like a desert."

I smiled. "I guess in contrast to central Luzon, it does seem rather dry, doesn't it?"

"That's an understatement!"

We continued to chat and catch up on our lives until I finally swung my car into the driveway.

"Welcome to my humble abode," I announced, as I turned off the engine. I hoped Estelle liked it as much as I did. It was a simple concrete-block structure, painted white, with windows on all sides. A bright-red, welcoming front door added some color. A two-car garage was attached to one end. There was also a small area around the house with cut grass and some small bushes hugging the walls.

"You live here . . . all by yourself?" Estelle asked. She seemed amazed. "It's so big!"

I tried to see my home through her eyes. In comparison, it was a lot larger than any of the places she had lived. "Yes, once my husband Bob and my mother died, I've lived here alone. Come on in and see the inside. I turned the heat up to make you comfortable."

She shivered. "Thank you. It's freezing here."

After we carried her bags into the house, I thought of what I wanted to ask her before I could forget again. "Estelle, do you remember the number on the holding account I apparently have? The bank manager said I would need that for access to the account."

"But I gave it to you," Estelle said. "In that big envelope we stuffed with your Philippine maps and pretty pictures that we mailed at the airport."

I sat down and pushed back into my chair. "Now where did that go? That was when I wanted to forget everything about that trip. I thought I'd lost you, and it hurt so much. I must have put it out of sight."

Or maybe Aunt Frances stashed it someplace.

"Just forget that for now, Sue, I'm so tired. I really need to take a shower. I feel like I've been in the same clothes for days."

"I've got a room ready for you," I said. "You and Chris will take the bedroom behind the second door on the left." She followed me as I opened the door to a bright, airy room. "There's a bathroom door in there too."

While Estelle took her shower, I got up and started looking through drawers, on shelves, and then I finally found the large envelope in the hall coat closet.

Just then, I heard a loud screech from Estelle. "Sue! Sue!" Estelle yelled. "How do you work this thing? There's only ice-cold water!"

I found Estelle shivering outside the tub wrapped in a fluffy towel while the shower blasted out cold water. I shouldn't have, but I giggled. "Come here, and I'll show you how to get lovely hot water too."

I pointed to the large ball below the shower head. "This controls the water flow up and down and makes it stronger or slower." Swiveling the ball to the right, steam began to spread out into the room. "Now it's too hot, so swivel to the left to bring in more cool water to the mix. Ah . . . Feel that. Warm, not scalding. Have fun! You'll find out this is a new way of living." I remembered a similar statement from Estelle about kaingin-hut style conditions. I also showed Estelle how to flush the toilet.

Estelle giggled too. "I can immediately make a fire with no matches, but I can't even turn on a shower in America." Then they both doubled over in spontaneous laughter. Glad to be together. Glad to be experiencing life together again.

After finishing her shower, Estelle padded out into the bedroom with bare feet. "I never realized how good a hot shower feels. Almost as good as our own Lagmay swimming hole back home." She flopped down on the big bed.

"I remember one time when I'd gone with my dad clear into Cabanatuan and was waiting for him. I found a pretty blouse on a table piled with clothes they had just taken out of a huge sack labeled: USA RELIEF GOODS. I bought that blouse for only a peso. Wore it for years in college. I also found another shirt I wanted to take home and give to Joe. *We can skip lunch today to pay for it,* I thought. When dad found me, I asked, 'Dad, you'd like a new shirt, wouldn't you? Look through this stuff. It's only one peso.'

"Then I turned to look at a table piled with pocket-size books. I'd never seen so many books. Some books didn't even have covers. One little book caught my eye, though. I bought the first New Testament I'd ever seen and took it home to Joe." She pointed at my overflowing bookcase. "Those shelves remind me of that time." Estelle closed her eyes and yawned. "I'm so tired, and this bed is so soft. Mind if I go to sleep for a while?"

Before I left the room, she was sound asleep.

I walked into the kitchen to see what I could cook up for dinner that night. I'd forgotten how exhausting an international flight could be.

J.R. called from the airport, and I grabbed the phone before the ringing woke up Estelle. "Their luggage didn't come in on the same flight. It's expected on the next plane from Billings. We plan to wait here until then. Bye, till later."

THIRTY

Explanations

Powell, November 1981

Hours later, I laid down for a rest too. I woke when sleepy Estelle wandered in and sat on my bed. Wearing a set of flannel pajamas I'd left on her bed, she stretched her arms above her head.

"That sure felt good, Sue. Sorry to collapse on you. I just couldn't stay awake after that great warm shower." She looked around. "Aren't the men here yet?"

"No, not yet," I said. "Your luggage was delayed."

"Oh, then this is a good time for me to explain what has happened to you in recent months."

"Good. I've been somewhat confused, and pleased, by my own personal . . . What did he call it? Financial advisor or guardian of interest, I believe."

"That's right." Estelle scooted closer, eager to talk. "When it seemed we needed to protect you, Chris and I thought of his younger brother J.R. He's such an honorable man. He'd not yet found a significant place in our company. We didn't say anything about you, except that you were Joe's daughter. You'd never met, and we suspected that Sonny might try to harass you."

Stopping for a breath, Estelle continued. "J.R. was up to the challenge of a new place and also protecting the interests of Lagmay Enterprises." She giggled. "Also in protecting the interests of a lovely young lady. A really *available* lady, I might add."

"That nearly boomeranged, Estelle," I said, feeling my cheeks grow warm.

"What do you mean by 'boomeranged'?" Estelle's brows wrinkled in puzzlement.

I took a moment to think about how to explain it. "It's when something comes back to hit you. Let me put this better. In Australia, they have a bent wooden club called a boomerang that can be thrown and then return near the starting point. We use this as an expression about something you planned that turns out to be the opposite of what you intended."

"Well, what happened?" Estelle asked.

"I immediately thought J.R. was the man you were engaged to. I'd already become very friendly with him, dreaming of being with him."

"Ah, I can see how that would really have 'killed our kangaroo' . . . or something like that." I chuckled at Estelle's mixed metaphor.

"Now I have Chris," Estelle said firmly, "and I hope you have J.R. . . . or do you?"

"I hope so," I admitted, feeling shy. "Though nothing has really been put into words."

THIRTY-ONE

Numbered Account

Powell, November 1981

O nce I retrieved the fat envelope, I opened it eagerly. I found the little envelope Estelle had mentioned:

> *Dear new sis, Sue,*
>
> *At some time when we are apart, you will need this number. I can't say when or where. I can't even say why. Just know this is very important. Put it in a safe place, maybe your Bible, so you can produce it when necessary.*
>
> *Signed,*
> *Estelle de Cou*

She'd included a little calling card with a series of letters and numbers:

P. A. #JADC, EG14 (DRB) Philippines, SDC-G
431954 7855, 2456.

§   §   §

"The day I got up enough courage to enter the bank to do what Joe had asked of me," Estelle said, "I was just blossoming into a young lady. I may have been about fourteen years old. I was flattered by the attention of a man, not my dad. On one clothes-washing trip, Joe became serious.

"'Estelle,' Joe asked, 'would you do something very important for me and my daughter Sue?'

"'Of course,' I said. Joe held a few gold pieces in his hand.

'I need you to go into Cabanatuan with your dad and take these with you.' He showed me the gold earrings, bracelet, and necklace. 'And I want you to deposit them into an account for Sue in a bank. Don't even tell your dad. Make up some excuse about wanting to see what people there do—see what the city is like.'

"Your father was never strong enough to walk the several days out to the end of public transportation, where my dad loaded his fruit and crops for sale in the market. I realized I must do this for him since he couldn't.

"I was really hesitant, but Joe said this was very important to help his daughter Sue get money for college. Joe explained to me that he'd also wanted to start a prospector account himself.

"When I was about your age, some of my friends and I went panning for gold in the river. We actually found a few tiny nuggets. My dad said I should keep them safe at the bank. He took me down there and explained how to do open an account. Do you understand?"

I nodded hesitantly.

Estelle continued her story. "Joe said, 'Explain to the manager in the bank that accounts like this are being used in Montana and Wyoming in the USA. Nuggets are brought in by men to the bank for safekeeping. They are called prospector accounts. You could only deposit into them, and nothing could be removed for five years.

"The bank manager must have admired my spunk, as you say. My English was better than his. Anyway, he filled out the necessary card and number, took my little packet of gold pieces, and smiled. I don't think he ever expected to see me again. But he did, in fact, see me three more times. Each time, I made a deposit to the account and added on the years the money was in his control."

Looking at me, Estelle said, "I couldn't get at that account even if I'd written to you. So it sat there for ten years or more."

Now I understood.

ら   ら   ら

J.R. moved into my house, along with Chris and Estelle. It solved the transportation and housing problems until everything could be worked out. My house was plenty roomy, so it wasn't as if we were cramped at all.

J.R. and I still met to discuss money issues at the bank. Any time I spent with J.R. was becoming more and more enjoyable.

One day before we left the bank, I went to Steven Honor's office. "Steven, I have my prospector account number you requested."

"That's great! Let's take a look at it." He placed the little card precisely on his desk, examining each notation with his pen.

"Yes, yes, original depositor: JADC, trustee, Joseph Armstrong de Cou; EG 14 (DRB) trustee." He hesitated. His pen stopped at that point. Wrinkling his brow, he took down a book from the bookcase behind him. "Ah," he muttered. "DRB means Delayed Registration of Birth. Location—Philippines."

Smacking his lips, I thought he looked like he had just tasted the most delicious caramel candy. "Beneficiary—Sue de Cou-Gibson."

Meticulously, he continued going over each following number until he seemed satisfied.

I know why this man is a banker and not me. I'd never find that much pleasure in numbers.

Picking up the card that meant I was the beneficiary of a robust holding account, I smiled to myself. *In what way can I give to God's work from these resources?* I joined J.R. outside.

THIRTY-TWO

Aunt Frances Phones

Powell, November 1981

"**A**unt Frances calling," I heard as soon as I picked up the ringing phone. "Good to hear from you. How's life in frigid Wyoming? Are you getting any answers to your problem with missing Estelle? Are you back into teaching now?"

"Aunt Fran, I finally got a short letter. She apparently escaped her kidnapper, then hid until she could marry her man. They have opened a business together. She intimated that things were still dangerous for them, and that I should not answer her letter."

"Well, that's good news, isn't it, honey? I mean the fact she is safe, not that she is still in danger."

"And guess what? I don't need to continue teaching. A tremendous bank account has surfaced, which my dad set up when he was young. Then later he added to the account all those years I thought he was gone . . . I mean dead. This has been accruing interest since about 1944, so presently it's quite substantial."

"What! I'm so happy for you!" Aunt Frances exclaimed. "Now all you need is a great man to enjoy your fortune with."

"I may have found him," I said. "He's my financial advisor who is teaching me to understand how to invest my money wisely. His name is J.R. for Junior. A really nice man. We've become good friends and done a few things together. I have to help him buy a car, and even teach him how to drive it. He came from the Philippines and has never owned a car. I sure hope we can remain friends after those driver's training sessions. Aunt Frances, you should come down and meet him sometime."

My aunt replied immediately. "That I will do, for certain. If J.R. treats you as well as your Bob did, this will be a great new experience for you. Bye, honey, I'll call again."

ⓢ   ⓢ   ⓢ

In the living room one night after dinner, J.R. approached me. "What are you doing?" I sat working with a long fuzzy piece of yarn.

"I'm knitting a scarf for you, from lamb's wool, so you can remember those 'furry little beasts,' as you called them, at Clara's ranch." The needles continued to click together.

"You are a lot more domesticated than I realized when I first met you." J.R. sat down next to me. "I've noticed something else about you too. You are a controlled person. You have a spirit of calmness, except, of course, that first time on the plane. But even then, you weren't yelling out swear words, or calling out God's wrath on whoever wronged you.

"I notice you don't wear a crucifix as I do," he said, pulling the chain out from under his T-shirt to show her. "But somehow, you are a Christian even without it."

My hands stilled, and I laid my knitting in my lap. "I most certainly am. God's Spirit lives out in my life. God walked with me even through the horrible time following Estelle's abduction. My faith was stretched waiting for God's answer. I'm always looking for answers in God's Word, the Bible. Do you read the Bible, J.R.?"

"Not really. The priest at Holy Mother of God Church would read from the Bible, but in Latin, so I presumed we weren't meant to read or understand it."

"Listen to what I read this morning," I bent down to retrieve a piece of paper from my knitting basket. "This is from Isaiah 41:13: *'I am the Lord your God who takes hold of your right hand and says to you, "Do not fear; I will help you."'* I sure like to know God's got a hold of this right hand of mine."

J.R. took my right hand in his and nodded in agreement. "Teach me how to get hold of God's hand like that, Sue." *It was truly a God-filled, poignant moment.*

THIRTY-THREE

The Skeleton Speaks

Powell, November 1981

A little international news blurb, noticed by J.R. that month in the Philippine newspaper, caught his attention, and he showed to me.

I puzzled over it for a moment, then told Estelle to look on page six of yesterday's paper, datelined in the Philippines.

Estelle read for a moment, and then read the article out loud.

> *"In Quirino Province, the skeleton of a man, tentatively identified to be SOA, was found tied up in a sitting position in the door of his decaying hut. A Spanish medallion had been placed in the bony fingers of his left hand. Interestingly enough, in his right hand was a small crucifix."*

"Who do you think this is?" Estelle asked.

"Maybe this was a bizarre hint, left by some vengeful person, that what we hold in our hands cannot be taken with us when we die," I suggested.

Estelle, also very puzzled, said, "SOA must be Sonny Agra-viador. If he did this, he would not have left that medallion, that's for sure."

"Just before I left there, if this is our hut," Estelle said, "my parents had been clearing land for another kaingin. Your dad had a high fever and couldn't be moved. He died soon after. I planned to bury Joe holding his New Testament, but my dad took it from me."

"'Essie,' my dad said, 'Joe has read to us every day from this book. Now he can no longer read to us, so take this book with you to college and read to others.'

"That was a hard day of parting from my parents, from Joe, even from our simple home," Estelle said. "I packed up my few belongings, including the gold medallion Joe had given me, and left. One rather ragged little girl, with a large pack on her back, and a heavy heart. All alone. I cried most of the way to my aunt and uncle's house. But your father's New Testament has given me great comfort during all of my trials. It was because of your dad and his Bible that I gave my life to Christ, and I've never looked back. We are not only sisters because Joe was my teacher; we are sisters in the Lord. And He has kept us in the palm of His hand through all our trials."

My heart swelled within my chest, and we hugged each other tightly, knowing the truth of Estelle's words. God had never abandoned us, nor had my father.

Special Thanks

Many people have input into my book. I want to give special credit to Ridgley Hoyt-Whitaker, a friend who asked if she could read my book, after my comment: "Upon rereading it, it's better than I thought it was." I asked her to check the content and correct faulty grammar and punctuation with a red pen. Together we spent three years going over the manuscript. She prompted me to keep at it, when some weeks had gone by with no comment. I revised, revisited, and rewrote sections. Ridgley encouraged me through the process. My editor accepted my submission upon my first attempt.